◆ THE LAST HOLLYWOOD ◆ ROMANCE

A NOVEL

BEVERLY BLOOMBERG

BRIDGE WORKS PUBLISHING COMPANY
BRIDGEHAMPTON, NEW YORK

Published in the United States by Bridge Works Publishing Company, Bridgehampton, New York.
Distributed in the United States by National Book Network, Lanham, Maryland.

For descriptions of this and other Bridge Works books visit the Web site of National Book Network at www.nbnbooks.com.

First edition

Library of Congress Cataloging-in-Publication Data

Bloomberg, Beverly, 1950–
    The last Hollywood romance : a novel / Beverly Bloomberg. — 1st ed.
        p. cm
      ISBN 1-882593-36-7 (alk. paper)
        1. Television comedy writers — Fiction. 2. Television broadcasting — Fiction. 3. Hollywood (Los Angeles, Calif.) — Fiction. I. Title.

PS3552.L63964 L37 2000
813'.6 — dc21   00-023659
10 9 8 7 6 5 4 3 2 1

Jacket and book design by Eva Auchincloss

Printed in the United States of America

For Tom: love and laughter, sweetie pie

Many people in Hollywood were kind to me during my tenure there. Several of them are dead, which may be what happens when you're kind to someone in Hollywood. The ones who are still alive know who they are.

I thank Barbara Phillips at Bridge Works, for taking a chance on this novel. She was a relentless editor, and as soon as the scars heal, I'm sure I'll be grateful.

My sister Lynn Bloomberg read the very first finished draft of this story, because I knew she would only say good things. She did.

Elota Patton and Bill Johnson read almost as many drafts as I wrote. Michael Malone, at Yale, assured me it was publishable long before it probably was, and Victoria Pryor worked hard to make it happen.

My writing group — Joan Gleckler, Barbara Batt, Suzanne Blancaflor, Barbara Greenbaum and lost Susan Plonsky — insisted I return to the manuscript and finish it. They patiently disregarded my whining.

Necessary acknowledgment must also be made to my parents, who presented books as an essential miracle; to my sister Sally who inspires me still; and to my daughters, Eloise and Annie, who make the struggle worthwhile.

"Every story must have a begining,
a middle, and an end."

— The Mogul

◆ THE LAST HOLLYWOOD ◆
ROMANCE

CHAPTER 1 ◆ SHE TRIES TO MAKE A START ◆

I was late my first day of work. Way to make a fucking impression, I thought as I drove in.

I'd been unemployed for two months. I was doing okay; I had money in my savings account, and the Fiat was running all right for a change, but still, I'd been relieved to hear from my agent. "Mike Lanetti wants to hire you," he'd said.

"Great." Mike Lanetti was one of those names you learn your second day in Hollywood. He writes, produces, directs—everything. His production company currently had two shows in the top ten and untold pilots waiting in the wings.

"I don't know why he wants you," my agent said.

Thanks a lot, I thought. "What's the show?" I asked.

"Life With Lucky."

"That show's disgusting."

"Have you seen it?"

"No, but I've heard. "

"Emmaline," my agent said, "there are two kinds of people in town: the ones who are working, and the ones nobody talks to. Don't blow this job."

I've got to get a new agent.

The guard at the studio gave me directions and a temporary parking pass. When I finally reached Mike Lanetti's office, the door was closed and a woman at a desk sat guarding it. She had blonde hair pulled tightly back and penciled-in eyebrows. I tried to appear confident. I was wearing a fuchsia jacket and black miniskirt. At the last second, I'd put on this pink hat, a modified pillbox that held most of my hair tucked inside.

"Your name?" she asked.

"Emmaline Goldman Grosvenor."

She perused her list. After an excruciating wait, she located my name and made a firm pencil check next to it. Then she gave a pointed look at her watch, one fake eyebrow arched. I lied instinctively. "I had a flat tire. On the freeway. It's a miracle I wasn't killed. "

"You may go in," she said.

I opened the door. The office was decorator-contemporary, full of black leather and chrome. There were several men in the room; I was about to say *hi*, or perhaps even something witty, but I didn't get the chance.

"If Deborah Kerr married Fess Parker, she'd be Deborah Car Parker."

Huh?

There was a large ebony desk and behind it sat Mike Lanetti. He was in his late forties, I guessed, although it was hard to tell. His hair was dark and curly, shiny with styling gel. He had a long, squared-off jaw with a shadow of dark beard, and his shoulders seemed narrow and boyish in his charcoal gray pin-striped suit. He wore a large diamond stud in one ear and I was just about to introduce myself when suddenly, his body seemed to convulse. His head lurched forward, the veins in his neck rigid, his elbows pulled in to his sides and his hands clutched, white-knuckled, near his face. He was grimacing, making a gasping, shrieking sound. I found out later he was laughing.

See, Mike Lanetti has cerebral palsy. It's part of the whole legend: *Writer With Handicap Overcomes Adversity to Become Show Business King*—that sort of thing. I figured I could handle it. What the hell, I thought, I can be cool.

"If Betty White married Soupy Sales, she'd be Betty White Sales."

I crept further into the room until I could see who was talking. He was younger than Lanetti—maybe forty-eight, give or take a Hollywood five—pudgy, and he wore a white button-down shirt, khaki slacks and a navy blazer. Leaning forward, his shoulders hunched and his round face sincere and intense, he looked like the Pillsbury Doughboy trying to explain yeast.

I laughed. "Those are awful jokes."

"Thanks," he said. "Bud Goodman." Writers are suckers for anyone who laughs.

Then Mike Lanetti stood up and said, "Good morning, Emmaline." Only it came out, "Guh Dmowrnin, Gemuhlinuh." That's when I noticed the way his jaw seemed to be hinged sideways and his mouth had too many teeth. His body arched and jerked as he came around the desk; he looked as if he were being manipulated by some demented puppeteer. It was hard not to stare. He introduced me around the room, although I didn't catch much of what he said. He leaned against the desk, his long body continuing to jump and twitch in erratic spasms. He was wearing black-and-white Nikes.

"I wanted a chance," he said, and I slid onto a couch, "for the writers to get together first." He spoke haltingly; it seemed to take great effort for him to open his mouth and form the words. I had to concentrate to understand him and found myself nodding a lot. "No directors, no network liaisons, no actors. Just the guys who write the show." He pulled out a large blue handkerchief and wiped at his nose with it. It took him both hands to hold the handkerchief. "I hope you don't take offense, Emmaline."

"Huh?" I'd been caught staring. I replayed his words. *I howup you doan takah fance.* Take a fence?

"Take offense," Mr. Marriage Jokes, Bud Goodman, translated.

"At what?" I asked.

"You clearly aren't a guy," Lanetti said. His eyes protruded and his mouth pulled back in a skull-like grin.

I tried to smile back, although my face felt stiff. "Thank you," I said.

"We have a lot of hard work ahead of us," Lanetti continued. His voice was deep and the speed was distorted, slow and torturous. I went back to nodding. "I'm just a writer," he said. "Just like you. Except I'm richer." He cracked up, his giggle a high-pitched sucking intake of air. I looked at the other writers and they were all laughing, too.

Then the door opened and Eyebrow Woman wheeled in a cart with coffee and Danish. Mike lurched forward to maneuver out of the way. There was a glass slab coffee table in front of one of the couches; he banged his shin on the chrome edge twice before he got away from it. I couldn't tell if it hurt him or not. The way his face twisted around, it was impossible to tell what he was feeling.

He left. I see, I thought, the writers may be getting to know each other, but the boss is taking off. I lit a cigarette, got a cup of coffee, and started checking out *the guys.*

They were a pretty sorry lot. I recognized a team named Franks and Heywood—I'd worked with them on a

4

pilot at NBC. There was a fat guy in a red sweater, a little guy handing out coffee, a tall guy losing his hair, a skaggy guy checking out Lanetti's video collection, a token gentile type in Harris tweed, and Bud Goodman, who was inhaling a Danish. Jesus, I thought, who do I fuck to get *off* this show?

Ten minutes later, the door opened and Lanetti reentered, dressed now in tennis whites. He had a sweater tied around his neck and a racket in his hand. "I'm off," he said. They all stopped babbling and he was the center of attention again.

"You look like a bum!" It was Bud Goodman. "Before," he said, "the way you were dressed in the suit, that was nice. That was the clothing of a mogul. Now you look like an agent."

Lanetti grinned. "I'm playing tennis with Monty." Monty Newman was, I knew, the star of *Life With Lucky*. Hell, maybe Lanetti had a terrific backhand; I noticed no one came within range of his racket. "It's for the papers," he was saying. "They want pictures." The racket flew in a stiff-armed arc around his head.

"Pictures?" Bud said. "Can you beat it?" He looked around at all of us, I guess to see if we could.

"I do it for my mom," said Lanetti, grinning and twitching dangerously toward the coffee table again.

We all laughed, and I thought he was going to leave. Then he spun around and faced me. "I think you and mud should groom together," he said.

"What?"

"Mud Doodman," he said. At least, that's what I thought he said.

"Me. Bud Goodman."

"Oh. Right." I glanced at him, but then turned back to Lanetti. "What did you say we should do together?"

Mike replied with something incomprehensible, although the way everyone laughed, I assumed it was dirty. Then he gave us one last death-mask grin and lurched out.

Bud was the one who explained to me we'd be rooming together. Office space was tight, so the writers were doubling up. It could've been worse—I could've drawn the skaggy guy. I don't know how Bud felt about it. I never got around to asking him.

CHAPTER 2 ◆ NOW HE TRIES IT ◆

She followed me right into the commissary. That crazy girl Mike hired. I let her get in line ahead of me. Not that I was being polite or anything. I just felt better having her in front of me than behind me.

We stood there. Waiting for the line to move. Pretending we weren't looking at each other. Finally, she said, "Bud Goodman."

"Right." I knew what was coming. People always do it, ask me if Bud's my real name. I usually say it's short for Budarooney.

She didn't ask me that though. She said, "God, this food looks like shit."

Nice mouth on her. That wasn't the only thing, either. She was wearing this hat. Pink. With a veil, for crying out loud. I mean, come on. No one wears a hat in real life.

Plus which, she wasn't watching the line. There was a big hole ahead of her. I said, "Uh, the line is, uh . . ."

She moved up. Finally. Bought yogurt for lunch, that's it. I got my usual, steak sandwich rare, onion rings and two iced teas.

She was waiting for me by the cash register. She looked at my tray and said, "I admire your courage." I didn't know what to say. No one ever told me I was brave for eating.

Then she said, "You want to sit with them?" She meant the other writers. They were all sitting together. Writers do that.

If I was by myself, I probably would've. They're okay. Marvin Rudankowitz, he's a big fat guy. His partner, Joe Pfeiffer, he's skinny. Rudankowitz probably takes all his food. Leonard Neiderhoff, all he ever wants to talk about is the football pool. A team I didn't know, Franks and somebody. Another new guy, he was from New York, I think. Mel Biederbeck wasn't with them, of course. He's the head writer, likes to eat in the executive dining room. Or maybe he was on the phone to Monty Newman. Monty's the star of *Lucky* and he's also how Mel keeps his job.

The thing of it is, most writers are boring. They hang out on street corners rewriting pieces of paper that fall out of their pockets. They've all had lousy marriages. In my case, it's three. Well, two were lousy. The third one made lousy look good. Ba dump bump.

I didn't say any of that to her. What I said was, "We can eat outside on the patio if you want."

"Absofuckinglutely!" she yelled. It was all I could do not to change my mind.

The patio's nothing special. There's a wrought-iron railing. A few tables with chairs and umbrellas. You can actually see the Lanetti Mines from there. Down the alley between some soundstages. The best thing about the patio was no one else was out there.

"This is great." She was already at a table.

I said, "It's not much of a view or anything. Just the alley."

She said, "That's no alley, it's an escape route."

Was she being funny or what? One thing for sure, she was making me nervous. That hat. Plus which, I wasn't sure where to sit. Next to her? Across from her? I finally sat in the chair next to her, but first I moved it a ways. I didn't know what to do about the hat.

She opened her yogurt. When she stirred it some slopped over the edge. I said, "You have some, uh, yogurt . . ." She licked it. Right off the carton. I tried not to stare. "So, Emily, how'd you happen to come work . . ."

"Emma*line*."

"Huh?"

"Emmaline. I hate being called Emily." I remembered now, she kept repeating her name in Mike's office. Emmaline Goldman Grosvenor. Never trust a writer with three names.

She took out a pack of Marlboros and lit one. I waited for her veil to catch fire. I said, "You always smoke while you're eating?" She'd just started her yogurt, that's why I asked.

"Does it bother you?"

"No. I just, you know . . ." I wasn't going to say anything, but what the hell. "I just quit."

"Oh. Congratulations. How long has it been?"

"Since this morning. You know, the first day of the new season. Fresh beginnings. All that crap."

"That's nice," she said. "I'll put it out."

"No, you don't have to." I reached out to stop her and we collided, sparks flying all over the table. Plus which, she burned the hell out of my finger.

"Are you okay?" she said.

"Fine." It was my pinkie. I stuck it in my mouth.

"Here, have some ice. It's the best thing for burns."

"It's okay. Honest."

"Come on." She had a piece of ice all wrapped up in her napkin. I let her put it on my finger. It didn't look like I had a choice.

"Thanks."

"It was all my fault," she said.

"No, it wasn't, it was mine. I mean, it was no one's. It's fine. Really."

"Well, good." She sighed, picked up her spoon, twisted it around in the yogurt. I started my second iced tea. Then she said, "So, have you known Lanetti long?"

No one calls Mike *Lanetti.* "Long enough."

"Where'd you meet him?"

"Here."

"Here?" She looked around, like she thought I meant right there on the patio.

"L.A."

"Oh. You guys seem like pretty good friends."

"We're not going steady," I said. If she wanted to know something, why didn't she just ask me?

She said, "Did I say something wrong?"

"No. Why?"

"You have a funny look on your face."

"My mother's side of the family."

She laughed. But I still felt, I don't know. Strange.

You've always felt strange, Goodman. Ever since third grade when Dolores Brandeman said you looked like a bloodhound.

It's that stupid hat. I wish she'd take off that stupid hat with that stupid veil.

She said, "I wish I could take off this fucking hat with this fucking veil."

I stared at her, I couldn't help it.

She said, "You mind if I try smoking again?" She held up another Marlboro.

"No. I'll sit way back." She smiled at that. I said, "Why do you want to take off your hat?" I wanted to ask, And how come you said it right then?

"Because it's driving me ba-fucking-nanas!" She took a swipe at the veil.

I felt dizzy. I looked at her Marlboros, still sitting out on the table. I took a bite of my sandwich, but it was soggy. Finally, I couldn't stand it anymore. I said, "Why don't you?"

"What?"

"Take off your hat."

"Because I have weird hair."

"Oh." I looked out at the alley. An escape route, she'd called it.

Then she said, "What the fuck." She reached up and took off the hat. I saw what she meant about having weird hair. It was mostly big. It was reddish-brown, and it wasn't long, but it stuck out. She fluffed it up with her hands, which didn't help. She said, "There, does it look weird?"

"Yeah, sort of." I knew right away it was the wrong thing to say. That's the trouble with women. They ask you a question, then they get mad when you tell them the truth. I said, "It looks good weird."

"Forget it." She puffed on her Marlboro.

I said, "It seems hair like yours is real popular now."

She said, "Oh sure, nappy hair's always in." She was definitely p.o.'ed.

Then, I don't know why, but I touched it. Her hair. I stuck out my hand and felt it. It was soft. I didn't expect it to be soft.

I said, "It's better than the hat." I was surprised I said that. But I did feel better with that crazy hat gone. "You ready to go back?"

"I have to pee first, will you wait for me?"

She got up before I could say no. Plus which, I guess it seemed easier just to wait.

When she opened the door to go inside, the other writers came out. They were taking the short-cut back through the alley, still all together. She held the door open for them and as they walked by her, she suddenly bowed. Low. A three-musketeers kind of bow, rippling her hat through the air. She had a nice behind.

The writers stared at her. They were bumping into each other. You could tell they didn't know what to think.

Her pack of Marlboros was still on the table. I slid one out. Lit it up. What kind of idiot would quit smoking on the first day of work?

CHAPTER 3 ◆ BABY, IT'S A JUNGLE OUT THERE ◆

Tuesday morning, Mel Biederbeck, the head writer, summoned us all into his office for another meeting. Bud sat in a corner of the couch. I picked an armchair that looked comfortable but wasn't. A pretty Latina came to the doorway. "Anyone want coffee?" she asked.

Mel said, "I'll have a cup, Rosa. You know how I like it."

"I'll have a cup, too, Rosa," said Bud. "But I want it handpicked by Juan Valdez. He's one of *your* people."

She smiled at him indulgently. "I'll call Juan right away," she said and left.

Mel gave a fake cough and we all turned toward him. "People," he said, "the key to this season is planning." He was perched on the edge of his desk, and with his tweed jacket and suede elbow patches, he seemed to be going for the English professor look. It was undercut by the too-deep side part in his thinning hair. "We have a good preproduction schedule, ambitious, but realistic. All we have to do is follow my outline. What I like to call our Comedy Blueprint." He smiled expectantly. We waited.

He coughed again. "I know you're all eager," he continued, "to pitch stories and get started on your assignments. Therefore . . ." He opened a manila folder and removed some papers. "Rudankowitz and Pfeiffer?"

The fat guy in the red sweater, which he was wearing again today, raised his hand. "Here," he said. He took two pages from Mel and inspected both before he handed one over to the small guy next to him.

"Nyles Petersen?" That was the gentile, of course. I felt sorry for him: he'd drawn the skaggy guy, Leonard Neiderhoff, for his roommate.

"Franks and Heywood? I can tell I'm going to get you two mixed up." Mel chuckled and Tom Franks and Bob Heywood nodded wearily; they were used to being addressed interchangeably. "Bud?" Bud leaned forward, his arm extended, and Mel had to move forward from his desk. "And Emmaline." While he was up, he crossed over to me and ceremoniously handed over my sheet of paper.

Rosa came in with the two cups of coffee. Mel didn't bother to thank her.

"Now then," he continued, "I've spent several days developing these concepts, as well as tailoring them each to your specific talents. I think you'll find that every concept listed is a rich source of story material, in some cases, two parters."

Rudankowitz had his hand up.

"Yes, Marvin?"

"What if we have a really good story to pitch, one we know you're gonna like . . ."

Everyone laughed and Rudankowitz trailed off.

"I think you know the answer to that one, Marvin," Mel said with a tolerant smile. "Any other questions?"

I spoke up. I didn't raise my hand either. "Are we restricted to these lists for episode ideas?"

"No, of course not. I want you to use these lists as jumping-off points, that's all. Don't worry, people. We need *all* your ideas."

Rudankowitz raised his hand again. This time Mel just nodded.

"When can we start pitching?" Marvin asked.

"I don't want you to ignore these lists either," Mel said. "After all, these are ideas that Monty likes too. And Monty *is* the star." We all digested that, and then he added, "You can start pitching any time after tomorrow. Check with Rosa to schedule an appointment." Rudankowitz was already whispering to his partner. Mel stood up and said, "Okay, people, that's it. Let's have a good season."

Rudankowitz made a beeline for Rosa's desk. Bud and I went into our office. I held up my list and said, "This is lame-o bullshit!"

"You might want to close the door," Bud replied.

I did. Then, feeling foolish, I got louder. "It's fucking ridiculous! Listen to this: *wife beating, rape, spinsterhood,* old-age homes, *unwanted pregnancy, unwanted celibacy.* Fuck, what about *unwanted facial hair?*" I waited for my laugh, got none. "What'd you get?" I asked Bud.

"Mine's pretty good." He read off *unemployment, housing shortage, arson* and *rodent infestation* before he said, "Sorry, I guess I got all the funny ones."

"Is he serious?"

"Who?"

"Mel Biederbeck. "

"Mel's very serious," Bud said. "He never lets a joke cross his lips."

"How'd he get to be head writer?"

"He's Monty Newman's writer."

"Fucking politics."

"Uh huh." Bud had a pack of Salems in his pocket. He lit one, then carefully folded his list into an airplane, which he gently launched. It soared across the room and into the closed door, where its nose hit with a quiet *thunk.*

"You don't take it seriously," I said.

He shrugged. "Where'd you work before? I mean, you have . . ."

"Yes," I said, "I have been employed. I worked at *Linda Herscheld.*"

"Oh," he said. Most people are impressed, which they should be; *Linda Herscheld* is a high-quality show. "Didn't you have to pitch stories there?" he asked.

"What do you mean, *pitch?*" They'd used that word at the meeting, too—unfamiliar jargon.

"Pitch," he said with another shrug. "When you were working for Linda Hershfield . . ."

"Her*scheld* . . ."

". . . how'd they figure out who wrote what?"

I told him. "We'd start out with a policy meeting. Decide a progression for the season. Outline any new characters or themes. If you had a special interest in a certain show, you'd request it. The rest of the stories were divided up by the producers."

"It sounds civilized," Bud said. "Here, it's more like pigs fighting for slop."

"Does that little guy, Joe Pfeiffer, always twitch like that?"

"I wouldn't use the word *twitch*," Bud said. "That would be more Mike's department."

I was shocked. Was he making fun of Lanetti? He wasn't smiling. I said, "Where do you think Mel got these lists?" I waved mine.

"Probably looked in the dictionary under *comedy*."

"They had our names on them. And that bullshit about tailoring them to our individual talents. Do you really know more about rodent infestation than Nyles Petersen?"

"I do know a lot of rats," Bud said.

I lit a cigarette, then went over and looked out our window; we had a lovely view of the parking lot.

"Your list is the only one that makes sense," Bud said. "You got the woman's point of view."

I realized it as soon as he said it, then felt stupid because I hadn't seen it sooner. "Maybe I'll pitch Lucky getting pregnant. Then he can have an abortion. Kill two birds with one stone."

"May be too much comedy for Mel to handle."

"Shit. Shit, shit, shit."

Bud looked at his watch. "They don't start serving lunch till 11:45. A half hour." He sounded positively mournful.

It's funny how the so-called creative mind works. One minute I was feeling sorry for myself; as the only woman on the show, they'd given me this pitiful load of female crap. Then, I suddenly remembered this old *Andy Griffith* episode. Everything in TV is a rehash of something else anyway, and this truly appealed to my sense of sarcasm.

"Listen," I said to Bud, "what do you think of this? You know the hackneyed plot about the abandoned baby? Hero finds it on his doorstep with a note saying, Please take care of my child."

"What do you mean, *hackneyed*?"

"You know, *Andy Griffith* did one, *I Love Lucy*, everybody. What do you think?"

"About what?"

"For Lucky. He finds an abandoned baby on his doorstep. Unwanted pregnancy." God help me, it seemed perfect.

"And he thinks it's his?"

I hadn't thought of that. "Perfect. He thinks it's his. Not at first, at first he doesn't want anything to do with it, he's just going to call the orphanage or whatever, but somebody else says, Hey, Lucky, it looks like you. Who's another person on the show, somebody who could say that?" I'd only seen the show a couple of times. "Who's that cute guy?"

"Pete?"

"Right. Pete says it looks like Lucky and by the act break, Lucky's convinced the baby is his and he wants to keep it. What do you think?"

Bud looked skeptical. "I don't know. I'm lousy at stories."

"What about this for a really poignant ending: The mother shows up and Lucky has to give her back the baby. It's some woman whose boyfriend didn't want to marry her, only now he's changed his mind and he's going to. And of course, Lucky finds out it's not his baby after all. My God, he can go through all the bullshit of fatherhood and we can still get him back to the status quo in twenty-two minutes. It's perfect!"

Bud nodded uncomfortably. "Yeah. Listen, you wanna head over to the cafeteria? If we go now, there won't be a line."

I suddenly realized what was bothering him. Jesus, I can be such a jerk sometimes, especially when I get excited. "Bud, I hope you don't think I'm trying to steal your idea."

"Oh, no, I didn't think . . ."

"What about our writing it together? Obviously, it'd be a big help to me. You're familiar with the show. It might even be fun. The story's practically there, just a little more filling in . . . Bud?"

He was on his feet, struggling with his jacket. "I just remembered."

"What?"

"Dentist. I have to go to the dentist." He practically ran out of the room.

"What do you wanna do about the story?" I asked, but he was gone. By the time I got to the door and looked down the hallway, he was at the stairs. I never saw anyone in such a fucking hurry to get to the dentist.

CHAPTER 4 ◆ I WANT OUT ◆

I admit, I panicked. She started talking about writing together and I don't know. I left. I told her I had to go to the dentist. It was the best I could come up with.

The thing of it is, there was no way I could write with her. For starters, she's a real writer. Me, I'm a guy they keep around for punch-ups. Need a cup of jokes, ask Bud. Mel'd laugh me out of his office if I went in to pitch. They don't think of me that way. But her, that show she worked on, that Linda Hershfield, that's a good show. They've won Emmys, for crying out loud. How am I supposed to write with someone who won an Emmy?

I drove out to Malibu. That's where Joyce, my third wife, lives. After we split up she married this guy with a house out there. Gordon Vinelli. He's a screenwriter. Gordon's big claim to fame is coming up with those movies where the airplane crashes and the survivors have to eat each other.

I spotted Joyce right away. She was wearing a bathing suit made out of strings and little tiny patches of material. She looked good, even better than when we were married. Come to think of it, so did Linda, my first wife. Women always look good after they dump me.

"Bud, darling, you nearly scared me to death! You always were one for sneaking up on a girl." She was holding on to about a dozen of her bathing-suit strings.

"How you doing, Joyce?"

"I'm marvelous, Bud. Sit down."

I love that, *Sit down.* We're at the beach, there's not a chair in a million miles and she says, *Sit down.* Plus which I hate the beach.

"That's okay," I said. "I'll stand."

"Then could you move, just a teensy bit so you're blocking the sun? It's in my eyes." She had her hand up. Shading her view of me.

I moved. "This better?"

18

"Perfect. But darling, you look terrible. You have absolutely no color in your face. You simply must come out when Gordon and I have our next open-beach day. You need sun desperately."

I heard the kids laughing. That's who I came out to see. Edna. She's four. Almost five now, her birthday's September third. Joyce has a son, too, older. But I was crazy about Edna.

Joyce was still going on about getting a tan, so I said, "Thanks anyway. Skin cancer runs in my family." I knew that'd get her.

It did. She shrieked, "Bud! Must you always be so morbid?" Which was pretty funny, her calling me morbid. Considering her new husband, Gruesome Gordon. Besides which, she must've forgot I'm adopted.

I said, "Sorry, Joyce. You look great."

"Thank you, Bud. I'm not dancing any more, of course, so I took off some of that weight." Joyce used to be a belly dancer. She adjusted the patches of material. Made sure I got a good look.

I said, "So where's Gordon?" I knew I had to do a certain amount of this crap.

"He's in Caracas," she said. "Interviewing some people who were trapped inside a Corvair for thirty-six hours, buried under nine tons of dirt. Can you imagine?" She took a breath, and for a second, that's what I thought she was doing, trying to imagine. But then she said, "Or maybe it was nine hours and thirty-six tons of dirt."

Gordon'll find out, I almost said. But hell, Joyce doesn't have to let me see Edna. She's not mine or anything. I just like seeing her. The fact of the matter is, the reason I've stayed in touch with Joyce is so I can keep seeing Edna. So I said, "Gordon's a fine writer. Respected in the industry."

Joyce didn't even know I was lying. She said, "I'm so glad to hear you say that, Bud. Gordon and I are getting married."

I thought they *were* married. All this time, she could've been getting alimony.

She said, "I'm going to make this work, Bud. I really love Gordon. And the kids need a father. Besides, this is my fourth marriage."

She was lying. *I* was her fourth. But then Edna was there, hugging my leg, wanting me to pick her up. Nothing feels as good as a little kid's arms wrapped around your neck. She smelled like salt water and coconut suntan oil. "We'll see you later," I said to Joyce.

Edna and I walked down the beach. Checking out our footprints and walking in the water. I said, "You haven't called me in a while."

She said, "Mom won't let me. But I'm casing out a pay phone." I loved that, casing out a pay phone.

She told me about how she was learning Spanish from the housekeeper. She said when she ran away, knowing Spanish'd be a big help. I made her promise if she did run away, she'd call me. She said when she ran away, that's where she was running. To me.

I didn't stay long. It was getting late, and besides, I hated thinking about Gordon being her dad. But before I left, she made me get down on my knees. She looked me right in the eye. She said, "Do you still make flapjacks?"

I said, "I haven't made them in a long time. Not since I made them for you."

"Good." The way she said it, like she didn't want to share me with anyone else, made me feel better. She always makes me feel better.

That night I had a dream. I was at work. Emmaline was there and she was typing away on her computer and telling me I was supposed to use mine. I never do. I don't even like typewriters, why would I use a computer? Give me a yellow legal pad and a Bic pen and I'm a happy guy. Anyway, in my dream, there's Emmaline, typing away, yelling at me about being computer savvy, when who comes sweeping in with one of those food carts like they use in hotels? Linda, my first wife. And she's naked. Except for a nun's hat. Linda always loved nuns. She tried to become one after we got divorced. The last time I saw her, in court, she looked great. I said to her, "Linda, you look beautiful." She said, "I'm becoming a nun." I said, "I didn't know you could do that if you're divorced." She said, "Bud, you've always been so negative."

Anyway, the next morning, first thing I did when I got to the office was call Maintenance. Anything you want done, call Maintenance. Emmaline got in at 9:45 and they were almost through.

"What are you doing?" She was talking to the maintenance guys.

"They're taking my desk out," I said.

She hadn't seen me before, and now she whipped around. "Why?"

"We need the room. For the couch and coffee table." I got them out of the studio warehouse. "It'll be a lot more comfortable. Here, sit down, try them out."

"No, thanks." She was looking at the couch, frowning.

I said, "They took my computer out, too. I never touch one."

The movers were still standing there with the desk. "You mind?" one of them said. "This thing ain't no piece of cake."

"Great dialogue," I said when the maintenance guys were gone. "Ten bucks says he gives us a spec script. Hey, you want them to take your desk out, too?"

"No!" She practically ran to her desk. Protecting it, I guess.

"Suit yourself." I put my feet up on the coffee table. It felt all right.

Em sank into her chair. She looked miserable. Then she said, "I ran into Mel in the commissary this morning. I pitched the baby idea to him."

"Oh." I was all ready, had it all planned. I'd tell her I was hot on the trail of another idea, pretend I was working on my own story. She'd probably be relieved. I said, "About that whole thing, Emmaline . . ."

"He hated it."

I said, "Hated it?"

She said, "Abhorred it. He told me it wasn't a *Life With Lucky* story. Now what the fuck is that supposed to mean?"

This was great! "He say anything else?"

She sighed. "He said it wasn't my fault, I didn't really know the show yet. As if there's anything to know. An asshole hangs out on a street corner and other assholes bring him their problems. Deep shit."

Tell her, Goodman. You owe her that much, just as another human being.

It's none of my business.

Look at her: she's going to cry. You want to deal with that?

"Emmaline, it's none of my business . . ."

"What?" She looked up at me, her eyes all bright.

"You probably shouldn't have pitched it to him in the commissary. Mel likes to feel important. You can't feel important in a commissary unless you say no."

22

She sighed again, then she nodded. "You're right. I should've waited. I was excited. And it seems like such bullshit to have to make an appointment."

"That's Mel's favorite part," I said. The truth of the matter is, Mel's favorite part is pretending he's brilliant. He likes to think he's Arthur Miller or something. Which is what I was thinking.

When she said, "Fucking road-company Arthur Miller."

I almost choked. "Pardon me?"

"I said, he's an asshole who thinks he's Arthur Miller. The playwright."

"I know." It was a good thing I was sitting down. Why was I thinking of Arthur Miller? I *never* think of Arthur Miller. And what made *her* think of Arthur Miller?

Then she said, "So what do we do now?"

What'd she mean, we? I said, "I'm off to the dentist."

"Again?"

"Yeah, I have rotten teeth. Curse of the Goodmans." I was already at the door.

She said, "You want to kick around some other ideas?"

I said, "I wish I could." Sure I do. "Bridgework though. Could take weeks."

If something happens once and it's strange, like someone saying exactly what you're thinking, like maybe they even *know* what you're thinking, and then it happens again, does that make it *twice* as strange? Or is it two *separate* strange things?

Who knows? Who cares? I was out of there.

CHAPTER 5 ◆ LIFE WITH LUCKY, PART ONE ◆

I hate not working. Actually, that's not true, I love not working; what I hate is knowing I'm *supposed* to be working and not being able to. I should have been in a pitching frenzy like Rudankowitz and Pfeiffer were, but my mind was a blank the size of Texas. Mel's list was so unceasingly stupid that every time I looked at it, I got pissed all over again. If he'd approved my abandoned baby idea, I could be writing it. Shit.

Even worse, I was alone. Bud apparently needed a lot of dental work. Too bad, it might've been fun bouncing story ideas around with him. Maybe I should just kill myself, I thought. Right after I go pee.

There were six offices in our side of the building, four for the writers, one for Mel Biederbeck, and the big one for Mike Lanetti. Outside our door sat Peggy Brown, one of the two assistants assigned to the writers. Peggy was chunky and smiled constantly. Even now, pounding her keyboard, she wore a determined grin. The other assistant, who was young and pretty and whose name I didn't know, sat between Franks and Heywood's and Rudankowitz and Pfeiffer's doors. Katherine Rheingold, Eyebrow Woman, was posted outside Mike's, where she could keep an eye on everyone. I'd already heard some fairly crude stories about her prowess at giving head. The worst rumors are always about the most-hated people.

All the office doors were closed. I left ours conspicuously open. Then, thinking about Bud's dental appointment and not knowing the policy, I changed my mind and closed it, too. The bathrooms were downstairs, and as I walked past all the closed writers' doors, I thought, They all have work to do. Everyone has work except me.

When I came back upstairs, I saw Rudankowitz bustle out of his office with a messy pile of papers and place it reverently on Peggy's desk. Suddenly I had a brainstorm. As soon as Rudankowitz was gone, I walked over to Peggy. I waited for her to stop typing. After a moment, she sighed, and flipped on her screen saver— Sylvester chasing Tweety Bird. "You need something?" she asked.

"Yeah. How would I go about getting copies of *Life With Lucky* scripts? Starting with last year's episodes."

"What for?"

"I want to read them."

"*Read* them?"

"Yeah. I thought it'd be a good way to familiarize myself with the show."

She touched her mouse and Tweety disappeared. As she went back to her typing, she said, "Teri's in charge of files." She rolled her eyes in the direction of the young and pretty secretary.

"Thanks, Peggy." I walked over to Teri, who was leafing through a magazine. "Teri?" I asked. She looked about nineteen.

"Yeah, hi!"

"Hi, I'm Emmaline Goldman Grosvenor." I could feel Ms. Rheingold watching us.

"It's so nice to meet you," Teri said. "You know, you're the first person who's introduced herself to me? I guess everybody thinks I should know who they are, but I don't. It's so hard when you're new and everyone else already knows each other."

"I know what you mean. Listen, Teri, I'd like to get hold of some scripts. Starting with the most recent episodes from last year..." Teri looked suddenly unhappy. She shook her head; I thought I heard something rattle inside.

"What's wrong? I thought you were in charge of files."

"I'm in charge of putting things *in*," she said. "If you want to take something *out*, you have to talk to Ms. Rheingold.

"Oh." I looked over at Katherine, who was studiously ignoring us. "Okay. Nice meeting you."

"Nice meeting you too, Emily."

"Emma*line*," I said, knowing it was hopeless.

"Right." She grinned and went back to her magazine. It probably took all her concentration to turn the pages.

I walked the three steps over to Katherine's desk.

"Yes?" She was examining a script and took great pains to mark her place with a pencil before she looked up at me.

"I guess you heard what I said to Teri."

"No, what is it?"

I didn't see how she could've missed it, but I repeated my request.

"What would you like the scripts *for*?" she asked.

"I'd like to read them." I tried not to sound exasperated. "I'd just like to acquaint myself with the show."

"Ah, I understand." She swiveled her chair around to a bookcase, pulled out a massive blue binder and handed it to me. "Here you go. We call it *The Bible*."

"You do?" I opened it, turned some pages. There were paragraphs with titles like "Muskrat Love" and "Money Is the Root."

"It contains synopses of every episode we've done. Enjoy!" Ms. Rheingold gave me what must've been her rendition of a smile. It was terrifying.

"Um, I'd really rather read the scripts, Katherine."

"That won't be necessary, Emmaline. Everything you need to know about *Life With Lucky* is right in there. In *The Bible*."

"But see, I need to get the flavor of the show. The style of the writing, how the characters talk. Maybe if I speak with Mike . . ." She practically gasped; I was obviously proposing heresy. "It's just, well, this is helpful," I said, hefting the binder, "but I'd like to read some episodes in addition. How would that be?"

Katherine sighed. "I'll speak with Mr. Lanetti," she said. "I'll get back to you."

"Well, like I said, I'd be glad to talk to him myself."

"That won't be necessary," she said.

Or possible, I assumed. She returned to perusing her script and I was clearly dismissed. You may now stop casting shadows on my desk.

I went back to my office and flopped down on Bud's couch with the Newest Testament. My favorite episode had Lucky convincing a woman whose husband had recently died of bone cancer to get a cat; it was called "Because Cats Have Nine Lives." Jesus, I thought, this shit makes Mel's list look hilarious. I decided that would be my opening line to Bud tomorrow. Assuming his dentist gave him time off for good behavior.

CHAPTER 6 ◆ IT'S NOT MY JOB ◆

We were in the office. I was fooling around with the TV set, which they'd installed yesterday. It's for the network feed, so you can watch rehearsals and stuff. But the maintenance guy showed me this switch you can flip so it'll work like a regular TV. I was trying to find something good.

All of a sudden, Emmaline said, "Hey, Bud, listen to this." She starts reading me this letter to Dear Abby. "I'm writing you because I have nowhere else to turn. I am a victim of physical abuse. For years, I have hidden the bruises and made up lies about running into doors, but I can't stand it anymore. Before you tell me to go to a shelter for battered wives, Abby, let me add one more thing: My wife is the one doing the beating. Signed, Ashamed in Cincinnati."

She looks up at me, real proud of herself "What do you think?"

It turns out she wants to pitch it to Mel. For the show. She thinks it's this great twist on wife-beating.

"Hey look," I say, pointing to the TV, "*The Big Sky.*" I was getting real good at changing the subject, which is what I did whenever she wanted to talk about stories.

She looked at the TV set. "Howard Hawks. Kirk Douglas. 1952. Terrible movie." Then she went out to make an appointment with Mel.

I turned the TV off. She was right, it is a terrible movie.

Five minutes later, she came back in all excited. Mel was going to see her. I gave her my dentist excuse. I have to admit, that bridgework idea was genius. She didn't expect a thing from me. And everything was fine till Mel stuck his head out of his office and said, real nasty, "I guess I'm ready for you now." All of a sudden, I felt bad Emmaline had to face him alone. So I went in with her.

She started pitching. But she only got about two sentences out before Mel was jumping on her.

"Are you saying it's the wife who's doing the beating?" Personally, I was surprised he got it that fast, but when she said yeah, he started ranting. "You're making a mockery of our show! What about our integrity?"

Integrity, for crying out loud.

She took it hard. Which, I don't know, for some reason bothered me. It bothered me even more when she told me thanks. We were standing back out in the hallway. I said, "I didn't do anything. I sure didn't help any."

She said, "At least you were there." She looked like she was going to cry again. I wanted to tell her it wasn't worth it, but I don't know, who was I to say?

Then she said, "I hope this didn't fuck up your dental appointment."

Which I'd forgotten all about. "Right. I guess I better be going."

"See you tomorrow?"

"Uh, probably so. For a while, anyway." For some reason, I felt like a heel. I walked down the hallway and it was everything I could do to keep from turning around and seeing if she was okay.

So do it. Turn around and look.

No. Better to just not think about her.

What would it hurt if you just went back up and told her, Emmaline, it's not a big deal if you don't get an assignment right away. Huh? You could do that.

29

No way.

Why not? Come on, Goodman. Give me one good reason.

She makes me nervous. Did you notice her initials spell EGG?

"Can I help you with something?"

"Huh?"

It was that girl, Sahndra, the receptionist. I'd stopped in front of her desk. I didn't mean to, but I did.

"Do you need something?" she said.

"A second act. On rye."

"Mr. Goodman, you are so funny."

I said, "You keep spreading that rumor." Then I headed back upstairs. What I was going to do was just plain and simple, walk into the office and say, Emmaline, it's no big deal if you don't get an assignment right away. Hell, look at me.

Perfect. I'm proud of you, Goodman.

I walked into our office and there she was on the couch. She was thumbing through that big *Bible* thing they give to people. And she looked at me and said, "Bud, tell me it's no big deal if I don't get an assignment right away."

Holy Jesus, this makes three times she's said what I'm thinking. Comedy of threes, for crying out loud.

Coincidence, Goodman. Pure and simple. Just like you.

Three times?

It probably means you're on the same plane, mentally speaking. Although it's hard to believe anyone but you could fly that low.

"Bud, are you okay?" She was staring at me. All I could think was I had to get out of there. And then Nyles Petersen walked in. I was never so glad to see anyone in my life. "Nyles!" I practically hugged the guy.

He eyed me, a little suspicious. "You two want to get some lunch?"

"Nyles," she said, "tell me it's not a big deal if I don't have an assignment already."

"It's not a big deal," he said.

See? He can say it.

"Do you have one?" she asked him.

He nodded. "I'm doing an eviction story."

"I thought Bud had eviction," she said.

"Bud has eviction for non-payment of rent," Nyles said. "I'm doing a story where some homeless people get evicted. From sleeping on a grate."

"That is funny," she said.

"Thank you."

"So you two have lunch," I said. "It's perfect." I was backing out of the office.

Maybe Nyles could help her. "You know," I told him, "she won an Emmy." He'd probably think that was a good thing.

CHAPTER 7 ◆ LIFE WITH LUCKY, PART TWO ◆

You know the Beatles song that starts out, "There's a fog upon L.A."? This morning we had one: a warm, cottony fog, blocking out almost everything. Driving the Fiat to work, even with the top down, I could only see what was directly in front of me. Cars would appear from nowhere, popping up out of the fog as if some crazed Detroit magician were pulling them out of his hat. I had to concentrate. It was hard, but I liked it. At least I knew what I was supposed to concentrate *on*, for chrissake. I longed for that kind of clarity at work.

Bud was sitting on his couch when I got to the office. There was a styrofoam cup of coffee in his left hand and an ashtray with a burning cigarette beside him. The way he'd had the office rearranged, he could've been sitting in his living room. His feet were on the edge of the coffee table and his knees were bent, a folded newspaper propped against them. He even had a magazine underneath the paper so the ink wouldn't rub off onto his khaki slacks. He was a very neat guy, Bud. Even his shoes were neat: he wore penny loafers.

I thought, I cannot take another day with nothing to do. I said, "I wish the fuck we had something to do."

"I *am* doing something." He flashed his newspaper at me and I caught a glimpse of the crossword puzzle.

"Rosa said Rudankowitz and Pfeiffer have already got three stories approved." I'd run into her in the bathroom.

"Mmm."

I'd finally been able to read some of last year's scripts; when they moved out Bud's desk, they'd emptied the drawers into the trash. Among the contents were several old scripts. They were terrible, but at least I had some sense of how the characters spoke.

"Where do you think Mike is?" I asked. "We haven't seen him in a week."

Bud didn't even look up. "He's probably having meetings."

"With whom?" God, I sounded like an English teacher.

Bud shrugged. "With the networks. Actors. Directors, producers, people loitering in the hallways."

"How come we're not having meetings?"

"We're having a meeting right now. Two people, it's a meeting. Three, it's a discussion. Four or more, it's a conference."

I didn't feel like joking. "This is a dumb fucking meeting."

"Hey," he said, "I'm getting a lot done." He filled in another word on his crossword puzzle.

I walked over to the window. We're practically the only people in the building to have one. It's horizontal, and the wall is cinder block, so it looks like a window in a concrete bunker, but the sill is precisely the right height for resting your elbows on and looking out at the parking lot.

I went back to my desk and got a cigarette; there was only one left. I was smoking almost two packs a day. I was sweating more than usual, too, and generally feeling as if someone else were operating my body. I knew exactly what it was: paranoia, spreading through my soul with all the charm and finesse of a yeast infection.

"I'm gonna go buy cigarettes," I said. "You want anything?"

"I could use a Danish. Cheese, if they have any."

Just in time, I thought, looking at my watch. Then I realized I had accomplished something in my two weeks at work: I knew the complete commissary timetable. And I thought I'd been fucking off

I paused in the doorway. "Open or closed?"

"Closed," Bud said.

"Right. We don't want anyone disturbing you." Then I felt guilty, being sarcastic with Bud. Until I realized he hadn't noticed.

Out in the hall, I glanced over at Mike's door, also closed. Katherine Rheingold looked at me; I smiled, she didn't. I walked over to Peggy's desk. She was typing furiously, as usual. By now, I knew I didn't have to wait until she stopped; she was the kind of genius who could type and talk simultaneously. The office was crawling with talent.

"Mike in?" I asked her.

"I haven't seen him."

"I haven't seen anyone. Maybe none of us are in." She laughed, just a little chortle. "I'm going over to the commissary," I said. "You want a Danish?" She wanted a jelly doughnut if they had any, and a cherry Danish if they didn't.

I started downstairs. I didn't get far though; the stairway was packed with people. I had to thread my way down, and although I said *excuse me* repeatedly, hardly anyone moved. The lobby was crammed, too. I almost killed myself on the last step trying to get past a guy with dreadlocks. "What's going on?" I asked him while I rubbed my ankle.

"We're auditioning," he said.

"Oh." I moved away quickly, but I wasn't quick enough.

"You work here?" a young girl asked, clutching at me eagerly. "Could you put in a good word for me? Please? I'm *so* right for this show, I swear to God, I'm perfect. I have experience too, see?" She held her résumé up in front of my face. "Maybe you've seen some of my work at Le Petit Théâtre on Santa Monica. It's really a great place, even if it is small. I mean, we do Chekhov and Woody Allen and everything . . ."

I took her résumé; it was the only way I could escape. I was heading for the front door when the wall opened up beside me. Actually, it wasn't the wall, it was a door in the wall, but it was covered in the same jungle-print-on-mylar wallpaper as the rest of the lobby and even though I must've walked past it a thousand times on various trips to the bathroom, I'd never noticed it before. But then, it had never opened up before.

A man stood there. He was tall, about six-foot three, with huge shoulders that filled the doorway. He had straight black hair and bronze skin. He looked like an Aztec warrior.

"Who's next?!" he bellowed.

No one answered. He was incredibly intimidating.

"You!" he yelled. He was holding a rolled-up script in his hand and he pointed it at me. "Get in here!"

I looked behind me, the classic move.

"Yes, you!" He grabbed me and pulled me into a smallish, crowded office. He slammed the door shut, walked briskly to the director's chair, pulled up to a table, sat down in it and wheeled around to face me. I started to move toward the other chair across from him, but he said, "Don't sit down! You're here to read, remember?"

"But I'm not . . ."

"I know, you're not prepared. I've been hearing it all morning. Your agent told you we were only looking for atmospheres and extras. That's true, but even atmospheres and extras have to act, I don't care what anyone says. I also keep a file on whosoever I like and toward that end, I must hear you read." He was gripping; I'd never heard anyone use the word *whosoever* in a sentence. "You can read, can't you?" He threw a script at me; I barely managed to catch it.

"Here, give me that," he ordered. I thought he meant the script, but when I started to hand it back to him, he said, "No, stupid, your résumé, give it to me." I was still holding the lobby girl's résumé and he plucked it out of my hand. "Okay, page ten, start at the top, you're reading 'Bunny'. Go."

I didn't. I wasn't an actress, for chrissake. I tried to tell him he was making a mistake, but it was like trying to put out a bonfire by spitting on it.

He said, "Look, I'm tired of you prima donnas parading in here and taking up my time. If you need to prepare, or whatever the hell you call it, go out in the hall and do it. But I want to tell you, you're wasting your breath with this method bullshit. This is TV, honey, what we need is instant character."

"Just add water?"

"Oh, and she's funny, too. How old are you, thirty-five?"

"I'm twenty-eight!" Normally I don't even care about that shit; I wouldn't have said anything if this guy weren't such a flaming asshole.

"That means thirty-three," he said.

"Fuck you!"

"Not me, honey, save it for the producers." He sighed dramatically, squinting at me. "Jewish bitch, maybe Italian." He wrote something on the girl's résumé, then looked back up. "That's it. Good-bye." He threw the résumé onto a pile and walked past me to open the door. "Who's next?" he screamed at the crowd.

I was shaken. I didn't go to the commissary. It was a quarter to twelve anyway, too late for Danish. I pushed my way back upstairs, ignored Peggy's hungry look and gratefully shut our office door behind me.

Bud hadn't moved: penny loafers, crossword puzzle, cigarette burning in the ashtray. Maybe it was a new cigarette. God, I was relieved to see him. I said, "You look wonderful."

"Thanks. Had my hair done while you were gone."

"I mean it. You look so fucking unflappable." I threw myself down on the couch.

"You, on the other hand, look downright flapped."

"I was harangued by a maniac. Can I have one of your cigarettes?"

He handed me his pack of Newports. "Wanna go off the lot for lunch?" he asked.

The crowd was still in the lobby when we left, but no one spoke to us. Outside, the fog had changed to smog. It was different. The fog had been soft and soothing, but smog is kinetic. It bounces all over the place and gets in your eyes; if you don't wear sunglasses, you can die.

Sitting in his car, I could feel Bud looking at me. "We'll go someplace we can get a drink," he said. "You've got to learn to relax."

CHAPTER 8 ◆ NOT ME YOU DON'T ◆

This weekend I got my first hint that something was up. Mogul moves.

Mike called me up Sunday to meet him at Monty Newman's for tennis. Which right off the bat surprised me. Not that he invited me—I've been up at Monty's for rewrites plenty of nights. But that Mike was going. He and Monty hate each other. Even beyond that producer-star thing. Just goes to show how you never know what's going on. At least I don't.

Monty lives in Encino. One of those mansions with white pillars. Of course, there's no furniture in half the rooms. Anyway, I show up and Mike tells me Monty's busy with his agent. That's nothing new, Monty loves to keep everyone waiting. Plus which, maybe he got extra points for sticking it to a mogul.

Mike started warming up. Hitting balls against the wall. He'd drop the ball, swing the racket. Two simple acts, so hard I could barely stand to watch him, and I've been playing with Mike for years. To drop the ball, he'd hold his arm straight out, elbow locked and rigid, his fingers squeezing the ball so tight you'd think they'd pop it. He'd bring his racket back, his face twisted with concentration. His fingers'd suddenly splay open and the ball would fall and the racket would swing and most of the time, sonuvagun, he'd connect. *Ping.* Then I'd run after it.

Out of the blue, Mike said, "I hear Ms. Grosvenor is making trouble. Mel called me last night."

Good ol' Mel. Emmaline'd been in and out of his office all week. Pitching more ideas. By the book, too, taking them right off his list, making appointments, the whole nine yards. He shot her down every time. She'd come back into our office, I mean, the times I was there to see her, looking mad and cursing. But mostly she was surprised. Like rejection was something new to her.

I said to Mike, "So what are you going to do about it?"

Mike said, "About her getting Mel upset? I may promote her." He gave me that grin of his. Which always reminds me of a little kid sticking his fingers in the corners of his mouth, pulling them wide and saying *Nyaaah!* Mike always looks like he's about to say *Nyaaah!* when he grins. Right now he said, "That's why I hired her. To make trouble."

I didn't get it. Why'd he want her to make trouble? And who for? I wondered how the hell I was going to find out. "Trouble?" I repeated.

Mike gave a big sigh. Acting very patient. He said, "Look, Bud, what do *you* think our misogynist star Monty's going to say about Ms. Grosvenor?"

Missogin-who? "You think I don't know what that word means, don't you?" I could tell it was nothing good.

"I think you don't need to worry," Mike said. "This is between Monty and me. Now." He shifted his racket. "Want some pointers on your backhand?"

The next morning, she beat me to work. First time in three weeks. She was standing at the window. We're the only writers in the building to get a window. Probably a mistake.

I was looking for a place to stash the *Playboy*. I had it tucked inside the crossword puzzle. Finally I dropped the paper, real casual and everything, on the coffee table. She turned around. "Hi," I said.

"Hi."

I couldn't see her face. The light from the window was behind her, coming through her hair. Which looked different. "Your hair . . ." I started to say.

"Yeah, I got it cut. Big mistake, huh?"

It looked redder than before. Softer, too. It was all in little curls around her head. The light made it look like a big, frizzy halo. I thought of that day I touched it. The day I told her it looked weird. The day she read my mind. I said, "So what're you up to?"

"Thinking."

I laughed. I guess I was nervous. But I mean, how can you stop thinking? Even if you want to, your brain keeps on churning. Telling you stuff you don't want to hear.

"What's so funny?" she asked.

I shrugged. "Who can explain laughter?"

She said, "My father always gave me shit if I said I was doing nothing. So I got in the habit, whenever I was doing nothing, of saying I was thinking."

I pretended it made sense. "So what were you thinking about?"

"Nothing."

I laughed again. That's because I didn't know what to do next. I put my hands in my pockets. Found a roll of Tums. "You want a Tums?" I said.

"No, thanks." She walked over to her desk and got a cigarette. "I ran into Rudankowitz this morning."

"That could be painful." But I was glad to be talking about something real.

"They're writing the opener."

"Figures." Mike was crazy about Rudankowitz and Pfeiffer.

"He was so smug. He asked me what I was working on."

"Marvin can't help looking smug. It goes with being fat."

"I'm never going to get a story approved."

Tell her, Goodman.

Tell her what?

About what Mike said. About how he knows Mel keeps shooting her down.

I opened my mouth. Her new hairdo made her look about twelve years old. I said, "I've never had a story approved."

"What do you mean?"

"This early. In the season."

"Oh." She nodded. Believing me. Before I could tell her the truth, there were two sharp knocks on the door. It opened and Enrique Carlos walked in. Leaving the door wide open behind him.

Reek's been around forever. He does the casting for the show. Plus a lot of Mike's dirty work too. A regular mini-mogul.

"What're you doing here?" he said right away to Emmaline.

"What're you doing here?" she said right back at him.

"*I* was transported by aliens," I said. They didn't laugh.

She said, "He's the guy who harangued me."

"Oh yeah." She did tell me about some guy who thought she was an actress.

He said to her, "You tried to make a fool of me."

I said, "Too late to be first at that." No one laughed. Again.

"Then you are Emmaline Grosvenor," he says. "Enrique Carlos." At least he didn't do the phony hand-kissing bit. I've seen him. Nothing's too low for a mini-mogul.

I said, "His real name is Enrique Carlos del Taco Bell." He hates that. "Better known to his amigos as Reek. As in a strong odor of refried beans." Going for the laugh again. Getting nowhere again.

"If you've finished insulting me, Bud, may I deliver my message and go?" That's typical Reek. If he thinks he's losing ground, he finally gets to the point.

I said, "I'm definitely not finished insulting you. That's a life's work."

He gave a big sigh and said, "Number A, Michael would like a list of all the stories you've pitched to Mel."

He's always saying things like that, Number A. I said, "For pete's sake, Reek, A isn't a number. It's a letter. Ten is a number. Also your IQ."

He glared at me. "I am not speaking to you," he said. "I am speaking to Ms. Grosvenor." He turned to face her. "Number two," he said, "after the reading on Monday, Michael wants you to join him for lunch." Then he gave this little bow. "Goodbye. Or, I suppose you'd rather I say Adios." He gave me a snotty look.

I said, "If you leave, you can say anything you want."

He snorted and waltzed out. Left the door wide open. I closed it.

Emmaline looked pale. Maybe it was the light. "Why does Mike want me to have lunch with him? And why does he want to know the stories I've pitched?"

This is it, Goodman. Time to tell her what's up.

What do I know?

Maybe nothing. But maybe the truth.

Uh uh. People in TV start talking about the truth, I get nervous.

Everything makes you nervous, Goodman. You're the only one around here who can help her. Do it.

And I was going to. Only then she said, "Please, Bud, tell me what's up. You're the only one around here who can help me."

So I said, "What makes you think anything's up? Just because Mike wants to have lunch with you? Even moguls have to eat. Hey, speaking of lunch, are you hungry? Let's go back to that place we went the other day. We can get a drink."

She wants to know what's up, let her read someone's mind. Someone else's.

CHAPTER 9 ◆ IF YOU'RE THE ONLY ONE GOING CRAZY, HOW CAN YOU TELL YOU'RE NOT JUST BEING PARANOID? ◆

"Mike's gonna fire me,"

Bud was immersed in his crossword puzzle. Without even looking up, he said, "You've got a contract, don't you?"

That didn't mean I felt safe.

"He won't fire you. Mike'd rather eat mouse doo than pay off someone's contract. "

"Mouse doo?" I repeated.

Bud shrugged. "I'm a writer. These phrases come to me."

He made me smile in spite of myself. I'd come in that morning ready to spend as much time as necessary obsessing about this lunch date with Mike. "What am I going to say to him?" I'd asked. "Tell him to chew with his mouth shut," was Bud's reply. Now, he suddenly said, "Look, there's nothing you can do about it, right?" He stood up. "So come on."

"Where're we going?"

"Shopping." He was already out the door and I had to hurry to catch up. It turns out the studio has a warehouse where they store furniture and props. It's where Bud got his couch and coffee table, and where, presumably, they'd taken his desk.

"What am I looking for?" I asked.

"I don't know," he said. "What *are* you looking for?"

"Truth, justice and the American way."

He led me down an alley. We passed a giant flat painted a perfect sky blue and filled with fluffy white clouds. Bud waved at the impossibly accurate fakery of it and said, "You've come to the right place."

The warehouse was enormous, but well-organized. We were given a clipboard to make notes on, and some tags to attach to whatever we wanted to claim. We wandered down aisles of couches and credenzas, past desks and file cabinets, dressers and vanities, labeled with the show or executive who'd had them last. Periods and styles intermingled haphazardly like the world's largest garage sale.

"So how'd you wind up here?" Bud surprised me by asking.

"What, in Hollywood?"

"Yeah. You from around here?"

"Northern California," I said. "I came down here with my husband, Ned. Ex-husband now. We met at Berkeley—he was a conceptual artist and I was a playwriting major."

"Playwriting?" He seemed skeptical.

"Yeah, pretty funny, huh? When I met Ned, he was working on this very prestigious grant studying the effect of artwork on dogs. Ned felt they were making some good inroads, especially with the shorthairs, until they got in this brouhaha over the dogs pissing on paintings. He was asked to leave, and to take one particular Great Dane with him. That's when he formed the Pisseurs. You might've heard of them. It made his career. He was mentioned in *Newsweek* and everything."

"What about this?" Bud had stopped in front of a giant moose head. "You were talking about Great Danes," he said. "I thought maybe . . ." I shook my head. "Okay, go on."

"Oh. Well, we rented this house in North Hollywood. It was horrible. Something like a hundred and two degrees every day." Ned found a studio and he'd go off to paint, but I was stuck out there. The heat was over-whelming, and the feeling of isolation was even worse. One day, I took a walk and the asphalt melted all over my shoes. I remember sitting in the kitchen crying, trying to get the asphalt off my sneakers.

"It gets hot in the valley," Bud said.

"Yeah." I hadn't thought about any of this in so long. "So, anyway, after we'd been here about a month, Ned ran off to Mexico with his paint mixer. She was seventeen. He sent me this postcard so I wouldn't worry. I didn't even know he had a paint mixer." At the time, I hadn't known what to do. I stayed in North Hollywood. Shit, I was immobilized in North Hollywood. I kept ex-pecting Ned to show up with some cheap present from Mexico and apologize, but he never did.

"You okay?" Bud asked.

"Yeah, I'm fine."

"What about this?" He stood in front of a long piece of dark-stained wood from which protruded sev-eral mannequin arms.

"A hat rack?" I asked, unsure.

"More like a hand rack."

"Too creepy."

We continued walking. Bud said, "So then what happened?"

"Well, one day, I'm at the bank, transferring funds to cover a check I know is going to bounce, and I run into this guy from school, Sammy Katz. Only now his name is Sammy Shannon."

Bud nodded. "I know Sammy."

"And I'm telling Sammy all about Ned and the paint mixer and he's asking me what I'm gonna do, and I'm like, I have no idea, and he says, I could get you a job easy, and I say, You mean easily, and he says, Exactly, you could write TV." I paused in front of a fake fireplace.

"So Sammy Shannon hired you at Linda Hershfield."

"*Herscheld*, yeah. I worked there for two years and then Sammy fired me. He said I should go get a job someplace else and prove I didn't need him. What about this thing?"

He came over to look at the fireplace. It had a carved oak mantelpiece and fake logs. There was an electric cord coiled neatly and taped to the back. "Look," I said, "I think it lights up. We need this in our office."

"Perfect for those cold winter evenings," he said.

"Exactly." I attached one of our tags and Bud made the notation on the clipboard.

"So then Mike hired you from Linda What's-her-name's."

"Yeah, sort of. I was out of work for a while. I did a couple of pilots. *Marnie's New in Town* and *Lynn's Loves.* That's where I met Franks and Heywood, on *Lynn's Loves.* Then, out of the blue, my agent called and said Mike Lanetti wanted to hire me. He'd read some of my scripts and that was it. He didn't even interview me first."

Bud didn't speak. He was just walking along, nodding.

Suddenly, I spotted a purple leather hassock. It was round, about thirty inches across, with an intricate pattern made out of brass nailheads. It was Casablanca meets Hollywood Boulevard and I was hooked immediately. When I sat down, the welcoming squash beneath my butt was perfect. It was on casters, too, and as I gave a little push with my foot, I rolled closer to Bud. "I love this!"

"Good," he said, nodding his approval.

"This was really nice of you to do," I said. He glanced at me. "It really helps to have a friend around here."

He shrugged, clearly uncomfortable. "Is it heavy? We can probably just take it with us." As he leaned down to pick it up, the top of the hassock came off, revealing an inside area upholstered in soft black velvet.

"A secret compartment!" I said.

"For secrets. You have any?"

"Everyone's got a secret. What's yours?"

His mouth opened but nothing came out, and there was a look almost of panic in his eyes. We stood there a moment. Was he embarrassed because he did have secrets or was he just uncomfortable being thanked? From the little I knew of him, I'd probably never find out.

He lifted the hassock with a grunt. I took the clipboard. "Come on," he said, "let's go."

Show business is weird, I thought. The question is whether it beats getting asphalt on your shoes.

CHAPTER 10 ◆ SHE SHOWED ME HERS, DO I HAVE TO SHOW HER MINE? ◆

I came out to California in 1972 with Linda, my first wife. We were twenty years old. We got married right out of high school. No one thought we'd make it. We didn't really think it through, think how hard it would be on Linda. She was from one of those big Catholic families.

I got a job working at this car dealership. That was the only thing we came out here with, a letter from my Uncle Phil to this guy he knew, Harry Wheeler. Harry Wheeler's House of Wheels, a Buick dealership in North Hollywood.

North Hollywood, huh? Probably right up the street from where Emmaline wound up.

I worked my way up with Harry. Started out washing cars and by the end of the first year, he let me try selling. It was a great time for Linda and me. It was winter, only no snow, no chains to put on. And Linda got pregnant. She was so happy. Then, one day, Gene Muncy walked into the showroom. He hadn't made a movie for a while, and he told me later a lot of people said he was making a mistake doing TV. Of course, his show was a hit right away. Pretty soon all the stars were doing variety shows—Carol Burnett, Dean Martin—but Gene Muncy, he had one of the first.

It was the end of the day, and all the other salesmen were gone. It was just Harry and me. And Harry said, Go ahead, kid, you take him. I recognized Gene right away, but I don't think Harry did. Harry was mostly generous when it didn't hurt him.

The thing about Gene, he was just this regular guy. I mean, yeah, he was a great singer and a natural comic and he deserved to be famous. Hell, Linda was crazy about him. But even though I knew who he was, I didn't let on at first. I didn't fawn all over him and make a big deal. And before I knew it, we hit it off. Making jokes back and forth. He liked that. He wound up buying a Park Avenue. Top of the line luxury sedan, and he loaded it, too. Electric moon roof, leather interior, V-8 engine. He came in the next morning to sign the papers and he said to me, out of the blue, Goodman, why don't you come work for me? I said, On your show? That was the first time I let on I knew who he was. And he said, Yeah, on my show. I need a guy over there who's on my side. So I did, I went to work for him.

For a while, it was great. I was making a helluva lot more money, for starters. We needed it too, with the baby coming. Gene liked me, he liked my jokes, too, even if nobody else did. The truth of the matter is, until Mike came to work on the show, I never got a single joke in a script. They put us in a room together, me and Mike. Funny, back then nobody knew what to think of Mike. He made them all nervous. He was hard to understand and his body was always jerking. But nobody wanted to come out and admit he made them nervous. So they'd kind of pretend to ignore the twitching, which with Mike is a full-time job.

The thing of it was though, Mike was funny. He still is. And all of a sudden, we started getting bits in the show. Somehow when he'd say, we need a joke about chickens, I could do it. I could give him ten jokes about chickens. It was a good time for me. I was happy, Linda was happy. That was around February.

In March, she lost the baby. It almost killed her. Not physically, I mean, but you know, emotionally. And nothing I said did any good. I told her we could have more kids, that was no good. I told her it wasn't her fault, that was no good. Hell, I was a kid myself, how'd I know what to say? She started going to mass a lot. It was kind of the beginning of the end. After a while, she went home to Chicago. To be with her family. She never came back.

Gene's show lasted another three, four seasons. Mike sold his first pilot—*Tanya's Tigers*, about this traveling carnival troupe. When he got the order from the network, Mike said to me, "You're the only guy I know out here who understands what loyalty is, Bud. If you want it, you've got a job for life." So I took it. And I followed Mike from show to show. New ones'd come in, old ones'd go out, and there I'd be. A job for life.

What I said to Emmaline before about never getting a story approved, that was the truth. At first, I used to pitch along with everyone else. Then one day Mike said to me, "Bud, that's not your job. That's not the kind of writer you are." And I said, "What kind am I?" And he said, "The kind who has a cup of jokes. I come to you when I need a cup of jokes." And that's how it is. Even if I wanted to be a different kind of writer I couldn't.

The thing of it is, I didn't tell much of that to Emmaline. When she asked me how I met Mike I gave her the quickie version. And she seemed fine with it. She liked to ask questions though, and that made me nervous. Which is why when there was a knock on the door, I jumped up like my backside had a built-in spring.

It was Mike's secretary with our scripts. The opener. They had bright orange covers and the title was *Lucky Learns a Lesson.* "I'm not going to blame you for giving us this," I said to her. "I know you're only doing your job. Which is exactly what the Nazis said. Not that you're anything like a Nazi. Although I do notice you like to click your heels together. Of course, so did Dorothy in *The Wizard of Oz* and nobody called her a Nazi. Your name is Rheingold, though, right? Which is German if I'm not too much mistaken. Katrina, Katrina." She started to say something but I kept going. "You know how Katrina got her job?" I said to Emmaline, who replied, "Do I want to know?"

"No one else wanted it. They say behind every great man is a woman. In Mike's case, you have to stand way behind or else he'll spit all over you."

Rheingold finally left. I was just sitting down on the couch, figured I'd see how bad a job Rudankowitz and Pfeiffer did on the script when Emmaline said, "How do you get away with saying those things about Mike?"

"What're they going to do, shoot me?"

She said, "Everyone's intimidated by him but you."

I said, "It's hard to be intimidated by a guy who drools." Which is true.

But she got all up in arms like she had to defend him. Which people always do. She said, "Mike's had to overcome so much." People always want to make a saint out of Mike. Which, the honest-to-God-truth of the matter is, that's the one thing he's not. A saint.

I said, "You don't get to be a mogul just because you wear a velcro tie."

She said, "What does that mean?"

I said, "Emmaline, even a crip can be a prick."

"Bud! That's a horrible thing to say."

"It's true."

"It's still horrible." She stood just as the door opened. It was Reek. She said, "I have to go pee."

He said, "Thank you for sharing." At which she smiled and left. Reek looked around the office and pointed at our new fake fireplace. "What is that?" he said. Like he was really insulted by it.

"We went shopping," I said. I got up and switched it on. The logs lit up orange.

Reek snorted and sat down on the couch. "Would you like to explain her to me?"

"Who, Emmaline?" Was he serious?

"Mike is obviously grooming her for something," he said.

"Maybe she's an Airedale."

"Well," he said, "there is that hair."

Reek never comes out and actually says what he wants. I know that's against the law or something in Hollywood, maybe everywhere, but you'd think every once in a while, just by accident, he'd say what he meant. I said, "Reek, is there a point here?"

And he said, "The point, as you call it, is that it is obviously up to us to protect her."

"From who?"

"Bud, we both know that Mel Biederbeck has shot down every story she's pitched to him."

"So? You think she needs protection against Mel?"

"Among others."

"Others like who?"

"We'll have to wait and see about that, won't we?"

"Is this from you or from Mike?"

"Bud . . ." He spread his arms out, like how could I even imagine he wasn't in complete control of the empire. Then, just when I was about to tell him he was pissing me off, he stood up. He said, "You realize when I say it's up to us to protect her, I mean you."

"I figured."

"Michael put you two together for a reason, Bud. There's no such thing as an accident."

"Except when Mike can't get his zipper down fast enough."

He shook his head like he was just too exhausted by how stupid I was. He said, "I assume you know your function here."

"Sure." Anyone need a cup of jokes?

52

CHAPTER 11 ◆ THERE'S NO BUSINESS LIKE SHOW BUSINESS BECAUSE NO ONE ELSE WOULD PUT UP WITH IT ◆

The reading was scheduled for 10:00. When I walked into the rehearsal hall at a quarter to, it looked like a cocktail party. Folding screens partitioned off an intimate corner of the cavernous space, and the lighting was soft and flattering. People stood around being Hollywood hip: making slippery eye contact while they scouted around for a better conversation. There were even potted palm trees in strategic spots. It looks like a set, I thought, and, of course, it was.

Almost incongruous was the long table. There were about thirty chairs around it, with bright orange-covered scripts laid out at each place. Boxes of sharpened pencils alternated with glass ashtrays down the center. A few people were sitting already. I wondered how we were going to read in this light.

I looked around for Bud. I'd had this idea we would somehow hook up and go to the reading together. Stop whining, I told myself. As I approached the buffet table with the coffee, a man stepped right in front of me. His toupee was a slightly different color gray than the straggly, frizzy ends poking out from underneath it. He reached for the Sweet 'n Low, and I noticed he was wearing an ascot. Definitely an actor, I thought.

"Hi," I said to him, "my name's Emmaline Goldman Grosvennn ..." He walked away, just like that. Thank you too, asshole. I took my styrofoam cup of coffee and found an empty place against a screen to stand. I lit a cigarette; you can't beat smoking for giving you something to do.

The crowd was in smallish groups now, three or four people to a clump. They'd stand and talk a while, then see someone they knew, wave, walk over and form a new clump. The movement was constant, easy and smooth, a human lava lamp. I spotted Tony Wayne, who plays Pete, one of Lucky's minions; he was distinguished on the show by being the cute one, and he was cute in person, too. He wore tight jeans and cowboy boots and he had a big movie-star grin. Adalbert Argus, who plays the old candy store owner, Pops, sat near the end of the table reading a newspaper. As I watched him, he looked up at me. I smiled.

"Quit smiling," he yelled. "It looks out of place."

I knew it was supposed to be a joke, but his voice was so loud it attracted other people's attention.

Then Mike came in. He was wearing a dark, three-piece suit that managed to look expensive and rumpled at the same time. Maybe it was the beat-up sneakers he always wore. He was trailed by Katrina, as we all called Katherine Rheingold now; she carried a steno pad and a mug with the word *Bitch* on it.

"Mike!" someone yelled. Someone else picked it up and suddenly there was a migration toward the door. They all crowded around, and for a minute I was worried; Mike's balance is precarious in the best of situations. He seemed okay though, working the room like a pro, his long jaw seeming to hinge sideways like it always did when he laughed, his forehead and eyebrows twitching to some unknown rhythm as he talked, his hand flopping like a giant salmon as people shook it. I watched, but I didn't join in.

I refilled my coffee cup and approached Adalbert Argus. He hadn't been part of the rush surrounding Mike either. "Mind if I join you?" I asked, warily.

"Not at all," he said. He even pulled the folding chair out for me. "I'm Adalbert Argus."

"I know." We shook hands. "Your name's almost as bad as mine. Emmaline Goldman Grosvenor."

"That *is* odd." He had long white hair combed straight back and a red, crinkly face. "You make it up?"

I shook my head. "My father wanted to name me after Emma Goldman, but my mother balked. They compromised on Emmaline. "

"Why would he want to name you after Emma Goldman?"

"To spite my grandmother. She was rich."

He laughed. He had a gratifying, genuine laugh. The woman who plays Betty, the next-door neighbor, joined us. She said she'd changed her last name, which was Shumsky. Now she wished she'd also changed her first name, which was Rhonda. "I always tell people to call me Ronnie," she said. "I've never felt like a Rhonda."

"I think you look exactly like a Rhonda," I told her. She had red hair, big round eyes, and was wearing fuchsia polish on her long, acrylic fingernails.

"But what does a Rhonda look like?"

Actresses love to talk about themselves, especially their looks, but you have to be careful. "Glamorous," I said. She seemed to like that.

Tony Wayne and some other guy came over. Tony was even cuter up close. I was trying to decide whether to introduce myself or wait for someone else to do it, when Tony Wayne pointed at me with his chin and said, "Who's she?"

"Leave her alone, you animal," Adalbert said. "She's mine."

"Where'd you find her," Tony Wayne said, "*laying around?*" He elbowed his buddy and the two of them laughed and started banging each other on the biceps.

"Her name is Emmaline," Ronnie told them in a maternal voice that clearly said, *Be nice.* She introduced them. The other guy was Rob Montez, the film editor; I recognized his name from the staff list.

He said, "So what are you? An actress or what?"

"They probably sprung a new regular on us," said Tony Wayne. "We're always the last to know." Then he looked down the table. "Maybe they're replacing Arnie."

Arnie Dish, I knew, played another one of Lucky's cohorts.

Rob said, "I hope he doesn't cry."

Tony Wayne said, "I hope he does." Then Ronnie told them they were awful, and they proudly agreed.

Adalbert put his arm on my shoulder protectively. "Ms. Grosvenor is a writer," he said. I wondered how he knew.

"Oh, they finally hired a woman," said Ronnie. "Are you going to be *my* writer?"

I hoped she was joking. "I think I'm just common property," I said. That set off Tony Wayne and Rob to pummeling each other again.

When they were done, Rob asked, "Where'd you work before this?"

"*Linda Herscheld.*"

"That's a good show," Ronnie said.

"Why are you here?" Adalbert asked. "Besides the obvious answer that you're being punished."

Before I could speak, Tony Wayne said, "Hey, Adalbrain, are you saying our show's not as good as that dumb Linda Hershfield's?"

"Not only am I saying it, Anthony, the whole world is saying it.

"Then why's *she* here?" said Tony. I was back to the third person.

I said, "I go where they pay me. You know, Have Laptop, Will Travel."

"Who are the other writers?" asked Rob.

I didn't get a chance to answer him. "Bud's back," Tony Wayne said. "I already talked to him." He proudly leaned his chair back on two legs.

"Where is he?" Ronnie asked. They all began looking around the room for Bud.

Adalbert said, "He's over there. By the food." And there Bud was, spreading cream cheese on his bagel.

"Yoo-hoo, Bud!" yelled Ronnie.

Yoo-hoo, for chrissake. Bud was probably cringing; he hated even leaving the office because he'd have to go out and talk to people. At least, that's what I thought. I was floored when he waved back to Ronnie, then galloped over and gave her a big hug. She left a bright red lipstick smear on his cheek.

"Did you have a nice hiatus, dear?" she asked him.

"I can't afford a hiatus," he said. "Time and alimony wait for no man. I pay so much alimony my accountant's got permanent writer's cramp. He writes more than I do. Which isn't hard, come to think of it." He raced on, pointing a finger at Adalbert. "I know what you did over hiatus. You went to the track and to dirty movies."

Adalbert nodded. "And not necessarily in that order."

"Those movies are bad for you," Bud said. "The candy's always stale. Look at you, Adalbert, a year ago you were a young man. You've wasted your health on some out-of-focus footage of filth." He looked at Ronnie. "Hey, you shouldn't be hearing this." He clapped his hands over her ears. "As a matter of fact, neither should I." He covered his own ears. "Lucky I was talking and not listening."

They were all laughing; they clearly loved him. Tony Wayne said, "Why do we need other writers when we have you?"

"So I don't have to work, you fool," Bud answered. "We've got a whole slew of writers. That's how they come, a gaggle of geese, a slew of writers."

"As a matter of fact," I said, "there's the slew now." I didn't mean to interrupt the flow, but I was facing the door and saw them come in. Tony Wayne almost fell out of his chair laughing. Everyone else sort of coughed and tried to keep a straight face. Bud waved merrily.

It was 10:15. I wondered what we were waiting for. A young blonde woman in red satin jeans walked over to Mike. She said something to him; he said something back to her, which she didn't seem to understand. Katrina Rheingold joined them. Holding Mike's elbow, she listened to him, then spoke to the young blonde, who nodded and left. Katrina then went over to the guy in the toupee, and Mike did his marionette lope to the head of the table. That was the signal; everyone who wasn't already sitting did so.

Bud had taken my place. Tony Wayne and Rob Montez were begging him for marriage jokes. The other chairs were all filled; the only empty space was at the foot of the table. I put my coffee down and dragged over a folding chair. I thought Bud looked at me oddly when I sat down; he probably felt bad about taking my seat.

There were two chairs at the head of the table. Next to where Mike stood sat the asshole in the toupee. Shit, he was the director. Katrina Rheingold sat slightly behind them, smoking and looking bored. Mike was watching the door; I followed his gaze and there was the blonde in red jeans. I looked back at Mike in time to see him nod. She opened the door. Mike raised his voice, "Ladies and gentlemen, Monty Newman."

The door opened wider and there indeed was the star of *Life With Lucky*, making his entrance. Mike flung his left hand into the air toward Monty, then banged it against his right hand; he jerked it away, then banged them together again. He was clapping, for chrissake. A couple of us picked up on it, and started applauding too, then the rest of them joined in.

It was my first close look at Monty Newman. He was tall, with dark, curly hair, and there was definitely something magnetic about him. He waved as he approached the table; he had a surprisingly attractive smile. He wore tan slacks, a rumpled purple Ralph Lauren polo shirt, no socks and expensive-looking loafers with tassels. He sat down and the applause stopped. Then he looked around the table and said, "Where's Chip?"

"Coming." A boy about eight ran up, a doughnut in each hand. He played a kid in the neighborhood.

"He didn't clap for me," said Monty, unsmiling.

Bud called out, "Dock his pay!"

"Goodman, is that you?" Monty yelled.

"No, I'll be here later," Bud yelled back and some people laughed.

"Now then," said Mike, and the room quieted down.

"Wait a minute," said Monty. He pushed his chair back and got up, walked to Mike and spoke into his ear. I tried to catch Bud's eye to ask him what was going on, but he was suddenly interested in reading the title page of the script.

Then Reek was setting up some folding chairs away from the table, and Mike was whispering to two guys in suits. They both nodded vigorously and stood up, took their scripts and went to sit in the folding chairs. Monty Newman returned to his seat. "Are we ready *now*?" Mike asked. He looked around the table and it seemed as if his gaze lingered down at my end. I even thought for a minute he was glaring at me. Of course, with Mike, sometimes it's hard to tell exactly who he's looking at.

Everyone was quiet, tense expectancy in the air. There we were, these two long rows of people at the table, Mike and I at each end, like the parents of a huge alien family. So I said, "Yes, dear. Will you ring for the soup?" The silence lasted a second longer, and then it just broke. People laughed, opened their scripts, drank sips of coffee. I thought, Who knows, maybe this'll be fun after all.

CHAPTER 12 ◆ I HATE READINGS ◆

I figured I'd introduce Emmaline around at the reading. No big deal. But people in Hollywood get insulted if you don't know who they are. Besides, knowing Emmaline, she'd want to shake hands with all of them. I think in her last life she was a beagle.

Only I couldn't find her. I looked upstairs and in the lobby and when I finally gave up and went in the rehearsal hall, there she was. Over at the table talking to Adalbert. He's a good guy, used to be a writer before he quit drinking. The next time I checked, there was a whole crowd over there. Ronnie, Tony Wayne, that hot-shot junior genius film editor, what's his name?

I was standing with this network guy. He kept going on and on, I could hardly eat. "The network wants Mr. Lanetti to know we are behind the show one hundred percent."

I said, "That's great. You're better off behind it than in front of it. Otherwise you might get run over. Ha ha."

"Ha ha." It was a great conversation. Neither one of us was paying attention.

"Yoo hoo! Bud!" It was Ronnie. I like her. She reminds me of Donna Reed. I waved my bagel at her. Excused myself from the network guy. And walked over to see what Emmaline was up to.

The thing about actors is, you can't trust them. They say they love you, you're the funniest guy they ever met. Then someone else comes along with a better wardrobe and they're gone. Which is why I hated to see Emmaline, at the very first reading, trying to get in good with them. That must've been what she was doing. Why else would she make that crack about the writers? They walk in and she says, "They look like a slew, don't they?" Like they were slimy, for pete's sake. And what's this *they* crap?

Plus which, there's the whole thing about where to sit. See, no one ever talks about it, but there's a pecking order. Mike, if he's there, is always at the head of the table. The director's next to him. We had a new one this year, a scarf if I ever saw one. Meaning that's where he keeps his talent, in his scarf. Anyway, next come the actors. Then the writers. Then, on the left, the associate producer and the girl who works for him. Across from them, on the right, art director, wardrobe, props. At the bottom end of the table, you get your techs—lighting and audio, engineering. It's always the same, thirty-two places. And if it fills up you're supposed to sit near the table. In a folding chair. In the correct area.

Emmaline didn't pick up on any of it. I looked around for Reek. He's the one who sets the readings up, makes sure the pencils are sharp and the teamsters don't eat all the doughnuts before we get there. He should be getting her to move. I finally spotted him standing by a fake palm tree. I went over to him.

"She's sitting in the wrong place," I said.

"I noticed." His voice was low and flat.

"Tell her to move. Explain it to her." He was good at that stuff.

"I stick my neck out for nobody."

"Wait a minute. What about all that crap about protecting her?"

"Let's just say I have new information." His eyes were looking around the room the whole time.

"Meaning what?"

"It's not clear. I don't want to say yet."

"And what if Mike is feeling like a mogul on the rag and decides to make an example of her?"

He finally looked right at me. "Do the words *sacrificial lamb* mean anything to you?"

"He's setting her up?" I couldn't believe it. Is that what this was?

"I knew that curly hair reminded me of something." He smiled. "Baaaaaaaa." Then he walked away.

I didn't want to, but I went over to her. "Emmaline," I said.

She looked up from talking to Adalbert. "Hi, Bud."

"Come on, it's time to move." I kind of jerked my head toward the other writers.

"I like it here," she said.

I looked at Adalbert. He knew what was up. I said, "Writers are supposed to sit over there."

"What, is there a seating chart?" She was laughing. She thought this whole thing was a joke. Then she said, "I'm going to get some more coffee. You want some?" Adalbert said no, and I shook my head. She went to fill her styrofoam cup.

I did the only thing I could think of. I sat in her chair. And I couldn't believe it. When she came back, she dragged over a folding chair and sat at the foot of the table. The one place no one's supposed to sit. I don't know why. No one ever asked why. Because no one ever did it. Until Emmaline.

My guess is the only thing that saved her was Monty making those network guys move. He hates them to even be at the readings. By the time that was over, Mike was sitting down before he noticed us all at the other end. Seemed like he looked straight at Emmaline. It's hard to tell, of course.

I saw Reek. He was back at his stand by the palm tree. I could tell he was waiting for Mike to explode, too. Only it didn't happen. Instead Emmaline made this crack about the soup. And everyone laughed, so Mike let it go.

We read the script. Got through it okay, considering how lousy it was. Arnie Dish yelled, of course, waving that cigar of his. No matter how many lines he gets it's never enough. Adalbert, on the other hand, he never complains.

We finished and Mike and Monty went off to talk alone. Which is what they always do. The new director made a speech. Reek announced a change in the schedule; the hiatus was coming a week later. "Talk to my agent," Arnie Dish said. "I don't do schedules." Emmaline doodled on her script.

Monty walked over to the food table. Mike gave us the sign, staggered a few steps away and all the writers got up. "Come on," I told Emmaline.

"Where're we going?" she asked. She's always got to ask questions.

Mike seemed disgusted, but then he always does after being around Monty. "The cast will start on the first act. That'll give them something to rehearse."

Emmaline was standing next to me. She said, "Something to reverse?"

"Rehearse," I said, trying to keep it low.

Mike heard me though. He wheeled around and glared at us. "We'll meet at 2:00. That all right with everyone?" We all mumbled. Times like this, it's important to blend in.

Except for Emmaline. She said to Mike, "Are we still having lunch?" With everyone standing there.

Mike lurched backwards. For a second, I got the idea maybe he'd forgotten about lunch with her. Not that you can ever tell what Mike's lurching about. He looked at her and said, "Yes, I suppose we are."

"Okay." She nodded. Then she said, "Also, I was thinking we could lose the whole second scene. Go right to the schoolyard. Tighten it up."

Silence all around. First of all, she's saying lose a whole scene. Even if the script is a piece of crap, you don't say it in front of everyone. Plus which, I could see her script. She wasn't doodling after all. She was making notes, for crying out loud.

Mike stared at her. Then he turned to me and said, "Bud, why don't you join us for lunch. If that's okay with you, Emmaline?"

"Sure," she said. Like she'd just won the lottery.

The actors started hollering for their lunch break and the reading broke up. When we left, the Scarf was saying something about getting them up on their feet. I followed Emmaline out of the rehearsal hall and into the lobby. I was trying to figure a way to ask her if she had any idea what was going on.

At the top of the stairs she turned around. Her eyes were all bright and she had this big smile. She looked like she'd been walking through autumn leaves or something. She said, "God, don't you just love readings?"

Nothing, Goodman. That's how much she knows.

I said, "Sure. Doesn't everyone?"

CHAPTER 13 ◆ IN WHICH I ALMOST FIND OUT WHAT A MOGUL EATS FOR LUNCH ◆

Bud wouldn't talk to me. We were upstairs in Mike's office and Bud was sitting on the couch, his eyes closed. Maybe he has a headache, I thought. I went over to the door and closed it.

"You better leave it open," Bud said.

"Why?"

"You just better, that's all." He sounded like a kid: *You better leave it open or I'll tell Mom.* But at least he was talking.

"Do you think Mike forgot about asking me to lunch?"

Bud opened his eyes and gave me a weird look.

"What's the matter?" I asked.

"Nothing." He sighed. Shit, is there anything worse than someone who says *Nothing* and then sighs? He closed his eyes again. I put out my cigarette.

I hadn't been in Mike's office since the first day of work. It was impressive, no doubt about it. One entire wall was windows; that was very impressive, considering the lack of them anywhere else in the building. The rest of his walls were covered with the typical, obligatory photographs. There was Old Guard Hollywood—Brigitte Bardot, Steve McQueen, Gene Muncy; Middle Ground Power Hollywood—Michael Douglas, Meg Ryan, Harrison Ford; and Up and Coming Youngster Hollywood—Gwyneth Paltrow, Leonardo DiCaprio, that skinny girl on *Ally McBeal.* For filler, he had Madonna and Bobby Kennedy. Mike was in most of the photographs. If you didn't know he had cerebral palsy, you might just think he was grimacing at having his picture taken.

The door opened. It was Katrina Rheingold, giving us each an icy stare. Bud kept his eyes closed, so she wound up back at me. "May I help you?" she asked.

"No," I told her. "We're just waiting for Mike."

"Oh." The syllable was crammed with condescension.

"Say," Bud said suddenly, "is your name Rheingold or Rhinestone? If it's Rhinestone, you might be worth something. How'd you like to be worth your weight in rhinestones? You could be the fattest person in the world and only be worth $1.98. Even Rudankowitz'd only be worth $4.95."

66

She finally gave up and left. I looked at Bud, who'd already leaned his head back and closed his eyes again. I wondered if I'd ever understand him.

Mike's phone buzzed and I picked it up.

It was Katrina. "Mr. Lanetti would like you and Bud to meet him downstairs. He says you're to use his private stairway."

"Thanks." I hung up, told Bud what she'd said. "Mike's got his own stairway?"

"Yeah." He stood up, stretched his arms over his head, then fell back into his normal, slump-shouldered stance. "Listen, Emmaline." He rubbed his face with his hand, sighed again. Then he fumbled in the side pocket of his jacket and finally pulled out his cigarettes. Every day he smoked a different brand; today it was Merit Menthols. He put one in his mouth. He lit it. "Emmaline, it's a good idea to prepare yourself for anything. We are dealing with the Mogul."

He was so serious, as if he were filling me in on some deep-rooted conspiracy. "It sounds like he's going to murder us or something."

"Emmaline. "

"Okay. I understand. Be prepared. The Girl Scout motto. Or was it the Boy Scouts? It doesn't matter, I belonged to both." I wanted to reassure him, make him laugh.

"Maybe we should just go," he said, with another heavy sigh.

Behind Katrina Rhinestone's desk, there was another door I'd never noticed. It opened into a stairwell. We walked down, emerging by the guard's booth at the back gate. "Pretty nifty," I said. Escape routes fascinate me.

Bud's car was waiting, Mike in the passenger seat. I had no idea how the car got there, and Bud didn't seem to care. He got behind the wheel and I climbed in the back.

"Let's go someplace we can get a drink," Mike said. His head was wobbling the way it always did; I wondered what the hell alcohol would do to him.

We drove toward Paramount and went to Emil's, one of those restaurants with oversized vinyl menus. Mike ordered a double martini. When it came, he brought a bent glass straw out of his inside jacket pocket. His big hands came together, the knuckles and veins straining as he gripped the straw tightly, moved it over the glass and dropped it neatly into the martini. He clamped his twisted lips around the straw, swallowed twice, and the martini was gone.

"Fucking A," I said, awed. Mike's arm was already over his head, signaling for the waiter.

"You ought to see him when he gets drunk," Bud said. "He walks perfectly straight." We all laughed and when the waiter came, Mike ordered another round.

We must've had lunch somewhere along the line, although I can't remember eating anything. I distinctly recall having five vodka martinis. I know Mike had six, and his were doubles. I remember raising my glass to him at some point and saying, "To my hero."

I did find him inspiring, and it wasn't only how well he held his booze, or how funny he was, when I could understand what he was saying. He did a Jerry Lewis impression that made me nearly wet my pants. No, all that was swell, but there was something else. Naturally, he attracted attention, what with C.P. and all, but more than that, Mike had power. I don't believe in auras, but

Mike had one, a regular Hollywood halo. And because we were sitting at the table with him, we were special, too.

During my third martini, Mike jerked back in his seat. His big chin quivered. "We're going to have trouble this season," he said. Actually, I thought he said *trouble this sneezing.*

"Trouble this season," Bud repeated for me. Mike nodded. I had just popped an olive into my mouth. Now I held it there, gumming it, as if I could hold off the trouble as long as I didn't bite down.

Then Bud said, "There's always trouble, Mike." Bud wasn't the sort to panic, which I appreciated. "You can handle it," he said. That's why you're the Mogul." I nodded eagerly and ate my olive.

"Oh, I know I can handle it," Mike answered, his arm arcing overhead for the waiter again. "I *like* trouble." He smiled. "I just wanted you two to know about it." I thought he was going to say more, but then the waiter showed up. "Hit us again," Mike said, a demented Doc Holliday.

I tried to concentrate on the show. Obviously, that's why we were having this lunch, to figure out where the trouble might be coming from. *Life With Lucky* was, I thought, a consistently bad sitcom; trouble might be coming from anywhere.

"Just remember one thing," Mike said. He was futilely trying to spear the olive in his glass and I finally stuck it with my toothpick and held it out for him. He chomped down on it, his teeth closing on the toothpick, too, so I had to tug hard to get it out of his mouth. He finished his thought. "Chaos is on our side." He spit a little piece of olive onto Bud's sport coat.

I know I nodded like crazy. I bet my head wobbled almost as much as Mike's. Bud was staring at me. I know Mike laughed that strange, high-pitched laugh he has. But after that, even though in the next few hours everything in my entire life changed, I can't remember another fucking thing.

CHAPTER 14 ◆ MOGUL MOVES ◆

When Mike told Emmaline and me there was going to be trouble, I wonder if he knew how soon it'd show up. I wouldn't put anything past him. He could've known all the gory details. And still sat there guzzling martinis.

It was almost three when we left Emil's. Not much lunch trade left, but what there was turned to look. We walked out single file, first Mike, then Emmaline, then me. She was pretty wobbly. Been tossing them back almost as fast as Mike. Not doubles, of course. No one can drink like the Mogul.

Outside the sun was glaring. What a jolt. Hide behind your sunglasses or you get retina burnout.

I was trying to remember where we parked the car when we saw one of those Hollywood things, a guy walking by carrying a pillar. Probably a prop from Paramount. Anyway, Emmaline said, "Look, a pillar of strength."

Mike looked at me. I said, "It's the liquor talking."

She said, "More like the liquor walking."

And Mike said, "Gee, repartee."

We laughed. We all felt good. Maybe for them it was the booze, but for me, I was just glad Mike liked her. When the valet guy drove up with the Buick, I was so happy to see him I said, "I love you. I'll never go to another valet parker as long as I live."

We got in the car. And Emmaline said to me, "You're the only person I know who makes jokes with valet parkers." She was looking at me in the rearview mirror.

Mike said, "Bud is an egalitarian humorist." He has quite a vocabulary, Mike does. He went to Princeton, I think—one of those Ivy League schools—before he came out to Hollywood. He said, "Bud's the Thomas Jefferson of jokes."

"Jokes belong to the people," I said. "And I wish they'd come pick them up." I was watching Emmaline in the mirror while I drove. It's a wonder we didn't crash.

"You *are* crazy," she said. Right at me in the rearview. Her makeup was sort of blurry around the eyes. It didn't look bad though. Sometimes a girl's makeup looks so perfect you get nervous. You might bump into her and smear her face by accident.

"You think I'm crazy?" I said to Mike.

"No way. You're the sanest person I know."

"Are you crazy?" I asked him.

He said, "What do you think?"

"I think I have the word of a crazy person that I'm sane."

Emmaline said, "We're the only ones who know." Mike laughed, a good mogul snort. I saw why he liked having her around. Mike likes it when people aren't, what's the word? Wary. Mike likes it when people aren't wary around him. Only I had this feeling that Emmaline couldn't be wary if she wanted to. Or needed to.

The first thing we saw when we walked in the lobby was Monty Newman. We couldn't help seeing him because he stood up. Monty's a big guy, six two. And all that curly hair makes him look even taller. His hair actually looks a lot like Emmaline's. I almost mentioned that, but something about the way he looked made me keep quiet. Which it turned out was a good thing.

"Hey, it's Mr. Comedy," Mike said. Pouring on the charm.

"Hey, it's Mr. Bullshit," Monty said back. Which is when I knew I was right to keep quiet. "You have a nice *lunch*?" He put a real twist on that word *lunch*. Like he was insulted just having to say it.

Mike said, "The caviar was canned." He was joking around. Maybe on account of Emmaline, who probably didn't know how much Mike and Monty hated each other. And two other girls were there. Monty's secretary, this tall girl wearing red satin pants, and the reception-ist, Sahndra. That's how she spells it.

"I don't think we've been introduced," Emmaline said.

For pete's sake, she was talking to Monty. She had her hand out, too. Monty gave it a quick shake. Didn't say a word to her, not even hi. Just right back to Mike, "That why you were late? You were out gang-banging the new secretary?"

Emmaline ignored him ignoring her. She said, "No, they were out gang-banging the new writer."

I looked at the two girls. I said, "She means me. I didn't give in though. I'm saving myself."

"She's a writer?" Monty said.

Mike nodded, his head lurching up and down. He said, "Emmaline Goldman Grosvenor. We got her from *Linda Herscheld.*"

Monty exploded. "Who cares? This script is crap!" He held it up so we'd know what he was talking about. "The show is crap and you're getting me girl writers?"

Emmaline said, "Sorry, I can't take any credit for this week's crap. I didn't write a word of it."

I thought Monty was going to kill her. His face got all red. It's one thing for him to say the show's lousy. That doesn't mean anyone else can say it.

I said, "Forgive her, Lord, she knows not what she does."

Monty said, "Why isn't Goodman writing something? At least he's funny." He was pointing the script at me now.

"You'll make me blush," I said.

Mike said, "Monty, as you've pointed out, we have a script to rewrite." He started up the stairs.

Monty yelled at him "Don't you turn your back on me, you little schmuck!"

Mike kept climbing. "I assume you gave your notes to the director." Calm and professional, every inch a mogul. Even on six double-martinis.

"This is breach of contract! The network gave me staff approval!" Monty was practically shrieking.

Mike whipped around so fast he lost his balance. Almost fell right into Monty's purple polo shirt. "Then go approve the network's staff, Monty. Because I sign the checks here. Including yours, as I recall."

Monty looked like he was strangling. "You'll be hearing from my lawyer!" he said. Then he stormed out. No one moved. Except the girl in the red pants. She ran out after him.

"What did he mean?" Emmaline. I don't know if anyone else heard her.

I said, "Did you hear his exit line? That guy needs a writer."

Mike looked at me. Then he looked around the lobby. Quite a few people had shown up during the shouting portion of the program. He said, "Ladies and gentlemen, I would like you to keep this discussion to

73

yourselves. If the rest of the cast, or the staff, or the network for that matter, find out that Monty Newman has walked off the show . . ." He paused to give them time to gasp. "It may cause a panic." He added, "And the last thing we want is a panic."

He gave one last sweeping look at everyone. And I could've sworn—I admit it's hard to tell—but I could've sworn that as he turned around, he winked at me.

CHAPTER 15 ◆ CHAOS IS ON OUR SIDE, SAYS WHO? ◆

My first thought when I woke up was that I had to puke. I opened my eyes. Emboldened by success, I looked around. I was in the office, on Bud's couch. The curtain at the window was closed. I heard a noise and was surprised to discover it was me groaning.

I sat up. There was a sport coat on top of me; it thundered to the floor with a crash. I switched on the lamp, trying to ignore the painful glare from the twenty-five watt bulb. My mind didn't exactly clear, but certain things began coming back: the martinis, for instance. Now at least I knew *why* I had to puke. I was determined, however, that if I did throw up, it wasn't going to be on Bud's sport coat. Not, I thought, after he was nice enough to cover me up with it.

I had to squint to focus on my watch; it was just after seven. At least everyone in the office would be gone. There'd be no witnesses to my disgusting condition.

I was wrong. When I opened the door and stepped into the hallway, every person in Hollywood was there. I was trying to figure out why, when Peggy saw me.

"There she is!" she yelled, pointing at me, and they all turned around, staring, completely silent. That lasted a nanosecond, then they all began yammering.

"Emmaline, what happened?"

"Did Monty really walk off the show?"

"Did you really punch him?"

"I heard *he* punched *her.*"

"What're you all talking about?" No one seemed to hear me.

"Are you glad you punched him?"

"I told you, *he* punched *her.*"

"When he found out she was a writer."

"A *girl* writer."

"Excuse me," I said, "I'll be right back." I held my breath and staggered to the stairs. I didn't puke on anyone. I was very proud of myself.

Then I ran into trouble. Enrique was at the bottom of the stairs. "You look like hell," he said.

"Thank you," I managed.

"Would you like to go into my office and talk about what happened?" His voice was low and calm, but I could sense the eagerness underneath.

"What I would like," I said, "is to go puke."

He put his palms up immediately. "Don't let me get in your way. Please."

I made it into the ladies' room. I looked in the mirror. In the fluorescent gloom, my skin was the color of dead oatmeal. My eye makeup, so glamorous this morning, was smeared and blotchy. My hair looked like an electrocuted poodle's. If I weren't nauseous already, I thought, this would do it. I went into a stall.

Then, after all that, I couldn't throw up. I leaned over the toilet. I *inhaled* over the toilet. I recalled a childhood chant about great big gobs of greasy, grimy gopher guts and mutilated monkey meat. I conjured up a photograph I'd seen once of a woman in labor, her face contorted with pain and the fetus all bloody and slimy. I recited some of my early poetry. Nothing worked.

Desperate, I stuck my finger down my throat, but all I did was scratch the roof of my mouth. "Fuck," I said aloud.

I went back to the sink and the fluorescent lights. I wet a paper towel, and after removing several layers of skin, managed to make some repairs to my makeup. I tried pinching my cheeks, but dead oatmeal is dead oatmeal. I ran my wet fingers through my hair; it went from poodle to Pekinese. All I needed was a little bow.

Upstairs, the horde had thinned out. The remaining souls were standing around smoking and putting out their cigarettes in styrofoam cups. I tried not to weave as I approached Mike's closed door. Katrina Rhinestone was on the phone, as usual. I waited. She put her hand over the mouthpiece and arched her fake eyebrows. "They're waiting for you!" she said.

"Oh." I went in.

Mike was at his desk; as I entered the room, he was blowing his nose. Enrique leaned against the wall, his arms crossed over his chest. The writers were littered around the room. Bud looked up at me for an instant. The director was sitting on one of the black leather couches and gesticulating wildly. "I wanna know why the fuck I wasn't told! How the fuck can I direct the fucking show if I don't know what the fuck is going on?"

Mike leaned forward, throwing both his arms on the desk for support. "Murray," he said, as if he were explaining something to a moronic sheepdog, "of course you're the director. No one is questioning that. Or the quality of your work."

It was a perfect remark, worthy of a mogul. The director developed an instant tic under his right eye. "Has somebody said something?" He suddenly sounded as if his scarf were too tight. "Has the network complained? They never liked me at the network."

"Sit down, Murray," Mike said. Murray wilted into a chair. "I didn't tell anyone about the situation with Monty because I didn't want to alarm anyone. Well, now it's time to be alarmed. And the question is, what are we going to do?"

Everyone had seen the treatment Murray got; they weren't about to open their mouths. They were all suddenly busy examining the rug and trying to disappear into the corners. Mike flung his hands up in the air and rolled his eyes impatiently. "Come on, you bunch of pencil-necked geeks! This is why I pay you big bucks."

Money was a concept they understood.

"I think Monty'll cool off by tomorrow, don't you?"

"He always has before."

"Why not write him out of this episode? Give him some time."

"Yeah. Monty can't be serious about staying out."

"He never has been before."

"He'll be back by next week."

"Definitely. "

I'd finally succeeded in catching Bud's eye and signaling him for a cigarette. He threw me the pack, which attracted Mike's attention. I felt compelled to open my mouth. "I don't think Monty's that big an asset."

Mike didn't answer, but Murray exploded. "Are you kidding? He *is* the show."

Rudankowitz snorted at me. "You can't have a show without a star!"

"I'm sorry," I said. I inhaled too hard on one of Bud's Merit Menthols and coughed.

Mike stood up abruptly. Twitching in his stiff-legged way, he came around the desk and then half-fell against the front of it. He was trying to lean into a casual pose, I thought. I noticed Enrique had moved slightly forward from the wall. "All right," Mike said derisively, "shall I tell you what we're going to do?"

They were all watching him carefully; Murray was transfixed. The Mogul said, "We're going to write a new show."

"You mean a new episode," Rudankowitz said.

"No, I mean a new show. Without Monty Newman."

"No Monty at *all*?" asked Murray. He could be forgiven; it was his tic talking.

"No Monty at all," said the Mogul.

"We could call it *Life Without Lucky*." That was Bud. People looked at him briefly, then back at Mike, wondering if they should laugh. Mike's face told them *no*.

He said, "I don't know what we'll call it. We'll figure that out later."

Enrique moved into Mike's line of vision. "Who's the star?" he asked. "You can't have a show without a star."

Mike grinned, his long jaw quivering on its crooked hinge. "I can make anyone a star," he said. "You should know that better than anyone, Enrique."

There was only one more question to ask and I didn't have to because Rudankowitz did. "Who's going to write it?" he said.

Mike scanned the room, his head trembling slightly. I thought, he sure knows how to create a dramatic moment. He seemed to be enjoying it, too; his gaze flickered over each of us before he tossed out his bomb.

"The writers of the new show," he declared, "will be Bud Goodman and Emmaline Grosvenor."

Funny: all of a sudden, I *could* puke.

CHAPTER 16 ◆ LIFE IS ◆

Life is a series of small humiliations ending in a large one.

I believe that. Like Mike. He decided Emmaline and I should write this new script. Like Emmaline herself. How the hell was I supposed to write with her when I don't know crap about writing in the first place? She'd figure that out in a minute and a half, blow the whistle to Mike. Which was maybe what this was about all along. Maybe I was the one being set up. More mogul moves.

I decided to cook. Bought some tenderloin on the way home. I put on some music. Make a roux for your ragout. I wound up having three glasses of wine. It must've been them on top of the Manhattans at lunch. Normally I'm not a big drinker. Just over two hundred pounds. Ba dump bump.

Ba dump bump. A while ago, one of those days Emmaline and I were killing time in the office, she'd asked me what it meant. I'd said it after some joke. I guess it's a habit. "It's a rimshot," I told her. "You know, from the old days. Burlesque. The comic'd make a joke, and the drummer would do a rimshot."

"And now?" she asked.

"Now I guess it's sort of shorthand. For saying a joke is corny. Or bad."

"And you think people need that spelled out for them?" she said. I wasn't sure if she meant to insult me or she did it by accident.

Anyway, with all the drinking, I must've passed out. Sitting right at the counter in a bar chair. The phone woke me up. "Yeah. Hello."

"Bud! You're a hard sonuvabitch to get hold of."

Crap, it was Harry. Harry's House of Wheels. "Hi, Harry."

"How the fuck are you?"

I said, "Great. Got enough money to last me the rest of my life as long as I die tomorrow."

"Always with the jokes," he said.

"Yeah, that's me." How's Isabelle, I wanted to ask. Not that I would. I rubbed my face. Lit a cigarette.

Harry said, "So, Bud, it's that time of year again. The new models are in."

I said, "Harry, I don't need a new car."

He said, "Look, I don't want any guff from you."

"I'm just saying you don't have to do this."

"I know I don't have to, you sonuvabitch. I want to. Not everyone would do what you did."

Not everyone would believe what I did. I married Isabelle for him. It was crazy, I mean, more than crazy, I don't know what I was thinking at the time.

It was five, six years after Linda left. I was working for Mike on a new show for Don Rickles. Harry called me out of the blue, invited me out to dinner. Isabelle was with him. She was something. French. Tall, blonde, she looked like some kind of statue. I don't know how they got together, but her visa was up and she was being sent back to France. Harry said the only way she could stay here was to marry an American. He was having trouble at the time getting a divorce from his wife. For starters, he kept forgetting to ask her for one. So I married Isabelle. Bad marriage number two.

Harry said, "It's worth a Buick to me, what you did."

"You're a generous guy, Harry."

"So what's the word? Another Riviera?"

"Yeah. That's fine."

"Same color scheme too?"

"Yeah, same everything."

"You're in a rut, you know that?"

I said, "Yeah. That's how I know it's me."

"Always with the jokes," he said.

When Harry finally got his divorce, he made a deal with his lawyer to throw in one for Isabelle and me, too. Then he told her she could pick out any car on his showroom floor. She chose a Riviera. On account of the name, which she liked. Being French and all. That was the last time I saw her. She handed me the keys and said, "You should get something from all this." Then she kissed me. On the cheek.

Harry said, "We can make immediate delivery on this car." Dealership talk. "Can you come in tomorrow?" Once Harry makes up his mind, he likes to move.

I said, "Yeah, I'll come by tomorrow. As long as I don't die in my sleep."

"That's not funny. Listen, I've got an idea. The wife's picking me up at two; we're going to a piano recital. You know I've got a five-year-old kid can play Bach?"

"I can't even play poker."

"So why don't you come by then? I know the wife'd get a kick out of seeing you."

Yeah, I felt like I'd been kicked. "No can do, Harry. Got to work. These shows don't get lousy all by themselves, y'know."

"Always with the jokes," he said.

We hung up. Life is a series of small humiliations, ending in a large one. Sometimes there's a large one in the middle too.

CHAPTER 17 ◆ MAY ALL YOUR CYCLES BE BI- ◆

I never have trouble sleeping. Even during my darkest hours with Ned, my ex, I could always find solace in sleep. Shit, sometimes I found solace for eighteen hours a day. But now all I could do was lie in bed, wide awake, and think about Junior Shapiro.

Junior Shapiro was the supervising producer at *Linda Herscheld*. Sammy, the old friend who'd actually hired me, was the line producer—he dealt with the unions, contracts, the technical side; Junior was in charge of the writing. He could be gruff and intimidating, but for some reason, he took me under his wing. When I handed in my first script, he called me into his office at the end of the day, poured us each a glass of bourbon, and said, "Good job, Emmaline. "

"Thanks." What writer doesn't love to hear that? He went on and I sat there, basking in the glow of his praise and bourbon. Until I thought I heard something else between the lines; I asked him about it.

"Well," Junior said, "it's nothing you should be concerned about. Standard procedure. Someone'll punch it up." I must've looked confused; I was, after all, still new to Hollyweird. "To add some jokes," he explained.

"Doesn't it have jokes?"

"Oh, this isn't a criticism of you," he assured me. "You're a woman. Women just aren't funny."

"What about Linda?" Linda Herscheld was generally acclaimed as the best comedienne of our generation. It said so in *TV Guide*.

"Miss Herscheld is my employer," Junior said. "I think she's very talented." Talented, but not funny: I didn't know it until then—you need a penis to be funny.

Mike had given Bud and me the assignment to write the new show, but he'd given us virtually no direction. Was he going to? There was supposed to be a whole new main character: how were we going to develop him? Especially if Bud kept ducking out of the office like he usually did. And what if Bud subscribed to the Junior Shapiro Penile Theory of Humor, too?

I got out of bed; it was almost six anyway. I took a shower. I got a couple of ideas and decided to go into work early and jot them down. If I had something coherent to show Bud when he came in, at least he would see I was serious about working on this script. Then my being funny would be a bonus.

By 11:30, there was still no sign of Bud, and the brilliant ideas I was so hot to write down barely filled half a page. I'd been concentrating for the last twenty minutes on compiling a list of possible names for the new character. I had six; none of them was anything I'd give a dog, much less an important, new, *funny* character.

I went downstairs to pee. When I came out, I noticed Enrique's door was ajar; on impulse, I knocked.

"Who is it?" he yelled, not entirely welcoming.

I went in. "Just me," I said.

He looked at me curiously. "Just you?" he repeated. "As in, you're all alone, or as in, you're insignificant?"

It was too complex for me. Or maybe it was too close. "Dorothy Parker used to answer the phone, 'What fresh hell is this?'"

"*Inferno? Ella no sabe qué Inferno es.*"

"I beg your pardon?"

He sighed noisily. "Never mind. Now, if you'll excuse me, I have work to do." He was standing at the far wall of his small, windowless office, thumbtacking up eight-by-ten glossies.

"Who are the pinups?" I asked.

"Callbacks," he said. "It's useful to have their pictures up when they come for interviews. Gives them a thrill." As I picked idly through the pile on his desk, he said, "Then if they get difficult, I do this." He took the photograph of a smiling brunette named Janine Eisenbach and ripped it in two. "It's very effective."

I watched him toss the pieces into the trash. "Wait a minute, you can't just throw her away." I picked the torn head-shot out of the wastebasket.

"Why not?"

"Oh, I get it," I said. "You have her phone number on file somewhere."

"No. Why would I?"

"What about her callback?"

He shrugged. "That's show business."

"That sucks."

"Like I said." He tacked up another eight-by-ten. "So, you busy writing?"

"Hardly." I was sorry as soon as I said it; you could almost *see* his ears prick up.

"Bud'll be in this afternoon." Maybe if I said it, it'd be true.

"Good," he said. "Let's go have lunch."

It wasn't like I had a full schedule. "Okay." He picked up his sunglasses and a buttery leather jacket. "I don't think you'll need that," I said, meaning the jacket.

"It's Versace," he said. "I *always* need it."

We went out to the parking lot and I asked if he wanted me to drive. "Where's your car?" I led him to the Fiat. He sniffed a bit, but he got in.

"Where should we go?"

"Let's drive for a while," he said. "Go left." I followed his directions and we headed up into the hills above Griffith Park. The top on the Fiat was down and the sun felt good. Enrique reclined his bucket seat. That's how you can spot a true Angeleno: exposed to sunlight for longer than five seconds, he instinctively lapses into tanning position. After a moment, he said, "So, the old Jews got you down?"

"What old Jews?"

"The old Jews who run Hollywood."

I smiled. "Mike Lanetti's not an old Jew."

"Sure he is."

"I thought he was Italian."

"Outside he's Italian. Inside he's an old Jew." I laughed. "Turn in there." He guided us to a deserted clearing. Then he took out his silver cigarette case and removed a joint. He held it up questioningly. "Do you imbibe?"

"Occasionally."

"Good." He lit the joint, inhaled deeply and then said, his voice tight with his breath still held, "Michael likes you. He thinks you're smart."

I took the joint. "Thanks."

"Are you?"

"What, smart?" He nodded. "Sometimes," I said. How smart was this, I wondered. Getting high with someone clearly in close communication with my boss.

"Writing this script is going to make you a very powerful woman," he said.

"I don't know about that."

"Well, I do. I know all about power." I was sure he did. I handed back the joint. "Power is like that jacket," he said, inclining his head toward his Versace, lying carefully folded in the back. "You know it's there, and I know it's there, so we can both forget about it. If I need it, I use it. But," and he raised his finger to make his point, "I don't *have* to use it."

"Reek, what the fuck are you talking about?"

"I'm talking about Michael. And I'm telling you not to worry. He's clearly grooming you for something."

"What am I, an Airedale?"

I thought he was going to make some crack about my hair, but he just squinted at me through the smoke. "How long have you and Bud been working together?"

"Counting what we've written so far," I said, "not at all."

"And is that a problem?"

"I don't think so." I tried to sound honest. "It's just hard to get going."

"Hmmm."

"What about you, has Mike given you any hint of what he wants this new character to be like?"

He sat forward abruptly, tamping the joint out and returning it to the case. "Where do you want to eat?" he asked.

"I don't know."

"Okay. Head back down the hill, I'll think of some-place."

I started the car and shifted into reverse. I was backing it out when Enrique said, "Just one more thing about Michael."

"What's that?"

"Watch out. As quickly as he builds you up, he can also rip you to shreds."

I wished he hadn't put the fucking joint away.

CHAPTER 18 ◆ FLASHES OF BRILLIANCE ◆

I've made some stabs at real writing. One time I wrote seven pages of a book. I would've made it to page eight but I started daydreaming. Imagining how great it'd be when my book was done. How I'd sign auto-graphs. Wear suede elbow patches. Borrow a dog for the photograph.

The thing about imagining is you can't always stop when you want. I even imagined the reviews my book would get. For instance:

> *Windows*, a new novel by author Bud Goodman, is exciting, riveting and human. Perhaps it is too human, for it fails miserably. Despite flashes of bril-liance, Goodman is unable to keep the elements of his slim premise moving. His characters are trite and his views of life absurdly outdated. . . .

Or this:

> *Windows*, a novel by new author Bud Goodman, is the sort of work a ten-year-old child would be ashamed of writing. Despite flashes of brilliance, the characters are absurdly outdated and the slim premise is trite. . . .

You'd think I'd be in charge of my own imagination. It didn't matter what I tried to write either. Like here:

> The opening of a Bud Goodman play is always an event for this theatergoer. I therefore approached his latest work, *Closed Windows*, with great eagerness. I was, quite frankly, disappointed in the extreme. Although still capable of occasional flashes of brilliance, Goodman is outdated and trite. Not only that, he is no longer slim. . . .

I work hard, too. On the reviews, I mean. Trying to make them come out right. I never can.

> Everyone loves a good time at the movies, but you'd better bring along the toothpicks if you want to keep your eyes open during this one. Called *Flashes of Brilliance* and written by Bud Goodman, it's a real dog. The night I saw it, the audience threw Raisinets at the screen. . .

First thing in the morning, I headed out to Harry's. Figured I'd pick up the new car. It was early, not even ten, so I knew I'd be safe. No way I wanted to bump into Isabelle.

Harry made a big fuss when I walked into the showroom. Called all the salesmen over. I could see they hated my guts. I used to sell cars, I know. They thought Harry was stealing their commission. They didn't know there wasn't a commission. I had some tickets to the show, so I handed them around. I figured if they're going to hate me, let them have a reason.

Harry took me upstairs to his private office. "Drink?" he asked me.

"It's pretty early."

"It's almost noon. Come on, what'll you have?"

What I was thinking was, Almost noon? It's 10:15. But that's not what I said. What I said was, "Bourbon. Lots of ice."

He gave me the drink, then he said, "I'll be right back. I've just got to close this deal. Nuns. Very big. If it works out, I could get the whole archdiocese." I looked around. Harry had the required photos on the wall. All the famous people who buy their Buicks in North Hollywood. Pretty soon Harry'd have a photo of the pope up there. Right next to old Angela Meyers with the big you know whats.

The door opened. That was fast. Maybe the nuns decided to shop around. I said, "Hey, Harry, this picture of Angela Meyers. How come you always go for the blonde with the big boobs?"

"Just good taste, I suppose." It was a woman's voice. Isabelle's voice.

I turned around and there she was. She had on a navy blue suit and white blouse. High heels, sheer stockings. I dropped my drink on the rug.

She smiled. "You are surprised to see me, no?" I forgot the way she did that, said "no" at the end of a sentence.

I said, "Yes. I mean, uh, how are you, Isabelle?"

She was still smiling. I never could tell what she meant by that smile. Her mouth would sort of curve over to one side. It made her look like she was making fun of the whole world. Except I was somehow in on the joke, too.

She said, "I am well. And you, Bud, how are you?"

"I'm well too. I'm real well." I was babbling. She kneeled down, started picking up the broken glass and ice cubes. Even that mess, broken glass on a wet paper napkin, in her hand it looked beautiful. "Don't cut yourself," I said.

"You need a new drink, no?"

"No. Yeah. Okay." It was something to do.

She made one for herself, too. Handed me mine. I drank some before I realized she had her glass out so we could toast. She'd given me scotch instead of bourbon.

She said, "I am here to pick up Harry. We are going to the piano recital of our son, David. Harry is devoted to the children."

I said, "Yeah. He told me."

We sat down. She crossed her legs at the ankles. She always sat like that. I'm no expert on women, that's for sure, but I know the word for Isabelle. Elegant.

"Bud, may I ask you something personal?"

"Sure." My voice came out squeaky.

"Do you ever think of our marriage?"

I drank some scotch. I hate scotch. "Sure. Occasionally."

"And what do you think? When you think of it?"

"I think . . ." What? What did I think? "I think I was crazy."

She laughed. She's got a great laugh. She said, "In Europe, the marriage of convenience is still quite common. Especially among the very rich."

I said, "Here it's just the very dumb."

"Maybe sometime you would like to find out what you . . . missed?"

Hey, Goodman, is she saying what I think she's saying?

"Would you, Bud?"

She is, Goodman. That's exactly what she's saying!

I said, "You want me to drop this drink, too?"

She smiled and got up. Slowly. Walked over to me. Took my drink. Set it down with hers on Harry's desk. Took my hand and pulled me to my feet.

Jesus H. Christ, Goodman, she's going to kiss you!

We both heard Harry at the same time. She was back in her chair smoking a cigarette when he walked in. He kissed her on the cheek and asked me if I was surprised to see her.

I said, "Yeah. Surprised is a good word."

He was in a big hurry. It turned out he had the time wrong on the kid's piano recital, it wasn't four o'clock, it was noon. Some devoted father all right. "Sign right here," he said.

"The last time you told me that I lost a wife." I signed.

Harry laughed. "Always with the jokes," he said.

When it was over Isabelle didn't say anything corny like "I hope I see you again." She didn't say anything. She was probably sorry for what she already said. If she really said it. If I didn't imagine it.

I watched her walk away with Harry. Me, I went to a bar.

The new car drove great.

CHAPTER 19 ◆ WHAT DOES A SPIC KNOW? ◆

The restaurant Enrique chose was typical Hollywood; if they spend lots of money on ambiance, you're not supposed to notice the food's mediocre. Our waiter was cute, blond and tanned. He recited five different house wines and I ordered the chardonnay. Reek ordered Perrier. "I never drink wine before two o'clock," he said. "It gives you wrinkles."

"What's the matter with wrinkles?" I asked.

"Are you going to give me that line about wrinkles giving a face character?"

"Maybe."

He sighed. "Emmaline, do you know the three great lies of Hollywood?"

"There are only three?"

He recited, "Your check is in the mail, Black is beautiful, and I won't come in your mouth."

I was shocked. "And add to that, wrinkles give a face character?"

"If the shoe fits. We people of color have more natural oil in our skin. Keeps us looking young longer."

The waiter arrived with our drinks. I ordered the lobster salad. "I guess you're paying," Reek said.

"We'll leave them your jacket."

"Sorry," the waiter said, "we're only accepting shoes this week."

"Gee," I said, "gorgeous *and* funny." I looked at Reek. "Maybe you should have him read for you."

Reek glared at me, then said to the waiter, "We're in a hurry." The waiter took his order and left.

I wasn't overly surprised at his behavior. "Why do you think people in Hollywood act like such shits?" I asked.

"Because they're spoiled brats and they think they can get away with anything they want. "

He clearly didn't include himself in that group. Or maybe he does, I thought, and he makes no apologies. "How'd you wind up working for Mike?"

"Oh," he said, "our families are old friends."

I knew that was bullshit. Peggy, our secretary, had told me that Reek did some kind of college-paper interview with Mike. Bud had told me that Reek started hanging around Mike during a hiatus; the next season, he had a job.

"And you do the casting."

"I do some of everything." He regarded me over the rim of his glass. He was a very attractive guy: late thirties maybe, with thick, black hair combed straight back. His skin was smooth, a cinnamon-brown color. His eyes were bloodshot. "What do you want to know, Emmaline?"

I shrugged. "I'm just curious."

"That's what you writers always say."

"That's because we hate saying we're nosy."

He smiled for an instant, showing bright, white teeth. Then it was gone and he was considering me again. "What do you think of Bud?"

"I like Bud." That was easy.

"He needs someone to protect him."

"From whom?"

"The same people we all need protecting from."

"You're losing me again, Reek."

"You'll find out. Soon enough." It sounded ominous, which of course, is how he meant it to sound. "You know, Emmaline, I'm nosy, too."

"What do you want to know?" I asked.

He waited a moment before he spoke. "Whether we're going to be friends or enemies."

The waiter brought our food, and I stared at Reek's crab soufflé. It's a terrible habit; I always want what someone else orders. The soufflé looked good, but it turned out to be soggy in the middle.

CHAPTER 20 ◆ WHO'S IN A NAME? ◆

I did my best to get drunk. The truth of the matter is, seeing Isabelle threw me. Having her try to kiss me threw me even further. Where I'd land is something I didn't want to think about. I didn't want to think at all. Which is how I happened to be drinking in the middle of the day.

After I knocked back a few, I figured what I'd do is quit my job. I'd had enough humiliations for one lifetime, let Mike screw someone else for a change. I was going to march into his office and quit. The only problem was I couldn't march. I couldn't even drive. The bartender got me a cab and I went home.

The doorbell woke me up. It rang a couple of times before I got my pants on and made it to the door. It was Emmaline. For crying out loud, that's all I needed.

"Hi," she said. "I was afraid you might be . . . are you okay?"

"I'm great. How'd you find me?"

"Your phone was off the hook. Your address is on the staff list and I just . . ." She trailed off and I knew she wanted me to invite her in.

"You want to come in?"

"Are you sure it's okay?"

Why do some people make everything so hard? "Yeah, come on in."

I call the place I live in the Nothing Manors. On account of all the places around me have names. Big names. The Westwood Arms. The Beverly Glenview. The Nothing Manors doesn't have anything wrong with it. Fact of the matter is, it doesn't have anything at all. Which is why the Nothing Manors fits.

She came in. It must've been about seven o'clock, because the sun was on its way down, slanting in through the living room windows. The light made her hair look halo-y. It reminded me of something, I don't know what. I said, "You want something to drink? I could make some coffee."

"Maybe I shouldn't have come," she said.

I shrugged. Maybe not, I thought, but that's not what I said. "I'm going to sit down," I said. I took the couch. I started looking around for my cigarettes.

"Here," she said. She had her pack of Marlboros.

I took one, lit it. So did she. Then she sat down in the armchair across from me.

"I didn't know who else to talk to." She looked really depressed. I know that look.

"It's okay," I said. "Just take your time."

She took a big breath. "I keep running into things I don't understand. I mean, I know it was stupid to get drunk at lunch with Mike. And God only knows what all that shit with Monty Newman was about. And now this script. Christ. I've never written with anyone before.

This morning I was trying to come up with a name for the new character, I couldn't even fucking do that. You've written on every show in Hollywood, you've probably written with millions of brilliant people. And it's a given you're funny. You are. And me, I never know if anything I say is funny."

I couldn't believe it. She was scared of writing with me.

Just goes to show you, Goodman. You can never tell what anyone else is thinking.

". . . And Junior Shapiro didn't think women were even capable of being funny. And I don't know, I mean, I don't think that's true, but I was thinking, maybe you do, at least about me. Which is possibly why . . ."

"Wait a minute. Did you say Junior Shapiro?"

She said, "Yeah. You know him?"

I said, "Sure. Junior doesn't think anyone's funny except him."

She looked relieved. Not just more relieved than I ever saw anyone else look. She looked more relieved than I thought you could look.

I said, "Hey, Emmaline, I think I've got a name. For the new character. Happy."

She thought a sec. "As in Happy Go Lucky."

"Perfect title," I said. She nodded. I just wished her name wasn't so long. I said, "You mind if I call you Em?"

"No. I mean, no, I don't mind."

"Good. You know, Em, I think this is going to work out." All of a sudden, I did.

She said, "Well, at least we have his name." She had a nice smile. Her top lip sort of flattened out, but nice. She said, "Names are always hard for me."

Nothing to it. All of a sudden happy was the way I felt.

CHAPTER 21 ◆ PEOPLE WILL SAY WE'RE IN BED ◆

Bud was hot to write; he wanted to work immediately. I was surprised, but, shit, I wasn't about to discourage him. I'd been waiting for weeks to get to work. Immediately was fine with me.

We called our new character *Hap* for short. He had to be as different from Lucky as possible. Between setting him up, establishing his relationship to the rest of the characters, and explaining Lucky's absence, we had plenty to play around with.

We worked for about two hours. We had a lot of good ideas, and most of the plot. Bud used all kinds of arrows and stars and he drew circles around important items. I like to use numbers; they give me at least the illusion of being organized. Bud thought that was hilarious. "The *illusion* of being organized?"

I said, "Sometimes the illusion's all you need."

"Or all you get."

We sat there for a second. I don't know about Bud, but I was wondering what to do next. I didn't want to leave, but we didn't seem quite ready to plunge into the actual script yet either. "Are you hungry?" I asked.

He pointed at his stomach. "You don't get a body like this by missing meals."

I was thinking about Dupar's; breakfast is my favorite meal. "You like Dupar's? They make great pancakes."

"Flapjacks."

"Whatever."

He said, "No, I mean, *I* make flapjacks. Pretty good ones, too." He jumped up off the couch and headed into the kitchen.

I should've known he liked to cook. His apartment was impersonal, the furniture looked rented, and the only artwork on the walls seemed lifted out of an airport motel. The kitchen, however, was a jewel. It was tiny, minuscule even, but fitted out and organized to perfection. Copper pots gleamed on wire shelves, gadgets of every conceivable kind hung from hooks, one entire counter was a wooden chopping block, and smack in the center of it was Bud. He looked happier than I'd ever seen him.

"What should I do?" I asked.

"Nothing. I mean, you can just sit there. This won't take long." He was getting out bowls, measuring cups, flour. Shit, he was making them from scratch.

I felt useless. I said, "I wish I had my laptop. I could start organizing our notes."

"I have a typewriter," he said. He'd already squeezed out of the kitchen and was rummaging around in his hall closet.

"I thought you hated typing. Computers. All that."

"I do." He backed out of the closet, lugging a dusty typewriter case. "My mother gave it to me." I'd never thought of Bud having a mother; now that I did, it seemed logical she'd give him something he didn't want. "I hope it still works," he said. It was an old Smith Corona electric. He plugged it in and the carriage banged to the left, then took a spontaneous tab-hop.

"Perfect," I said. So I typed while Bud cooked. I was on the second page when I noticed a sound, something besides the music and the drone of the typewriter. It was Bud. He was making a buzzing noise, sort of a simultaneous humming and whistling. He did riffs and everything. He was completely engrossed in his cooking. He didn't even look up at me.

Then he gave his wrist a flick. And the fluffiest, airiest, most perfect pancake I've ever seen floated out of the pan, did a triple somersault and parachuted back down to a cushiony landing. It was magic. I almost said something, but I stopped myself. It's so easy to spoil something perfect by talking.

I ate about thirty of those pancakes. They were better than Dupar's. I said to Bud, "I thought Dupar's made the best pancakes in the world, but yours are better."

"These are flapjacks," he said.

"What's the difference?"

"It's a comedy word."

He's serious, I thought. Then, suddenly, I got this inspiration. "Hey," I said. "You know what I think Hap should do for a living?"

"What?" We'd played around with several ideas—a vet, a plumber, a photographer—and we didn't like any of them.

"He's a cook!" I definitely had Bud's interest. I went on. "It could be a really neat way to show that nurturing side of him—he's always feeding people. Like somebody could be complaining to him about losing his job, and Hap says, You know what you need, and the guy says, Yeah, I need a job, and Hap says, No, you need some meat loaf and mashed potatoes."

"He could always be experimenting with new combinations," Bud said, getting into it, too.

"Perfect! Awful combinations. Oysters in peanut butter sauce."

"Comedy food!" Bud said blissfully.

I smiled. "You like it?"

He did. And the cook thing fit in perfectly with the story line we'd started: Hap was new in town, having come there looking for his cousin Lucky, who, of course, is temporarily out of the picture. He looks around for work, can't find any, gets embroiled with the locals—Pete, who's having girl problems, which it seems he did every week, and Ron, the character played by Arnie Dish, and Chip, the kid, and Ronnie, the voluptuous neighbor, and Pops, who owns the candy store. Eventually, it would turn out that Pops has a grill behind the counter and Hap would go to work there. We didn't even need a new set.

Bud and I worked well together, which I think surprised us both. I know it surprised me. He made a pot of coffee. The Smith Corona, antique that it was, did just fine. We started the opening scene. Jokes came; better jokes came. We made each other laugh and we smoked a million cigarettes. When I looked at the clock, it was a quarter to one; we were just starting the second act and I figured I'd go home after we finished the scene. Instead, we kept going and the next time I looked up it was 5:30. We'd written twenty-six pages pretty much without stopping.

"The fucking sun's coming up," I said.

Bud grunted. He was reading over my shoulder. "Wait, what if Chip says, We'll make this the Fluffernutter capital of the world."

"What's a Fluffernutter?"

"You know, a Fluffernutter. Peanut butter and marshmallow fluff."

"Yuck."

"You don't like Fluffernutters?" he asked.

"You mean it's a real thing? It sounds disgusting."

"It pretty much is," he said.

"How about some more coffee?" I stood up and stretched my arms over my head.

"How do you take it?" Bud asked from the kitchen.

"Black." Just like I have all night, I almost added, but I didn't. It was a funny thing, how Bud could notice the slightest deviation in the wording of a joke—if I typed a line wrong, he'd stand at my shoulder, repeating it until I got it right—but he'd lose his pack of cigarettes about three times an hour. He'd blush like a redheaded schoolgirl whenever I said *shit* or *fuck; crap* was as hard-core as he got. He was generous with jokes; he never claimed his punch line was better just because it was his. If he didn't like something I said, though, he wouldn't say *no* exactly, he'd just sort of pretend not to hear it. A couple of times I repeated a phrase to see what he'd do; he just kept pitching back new lines—all better.

"This was fun," I said when he brought the coffee over.

"Yeah," he agreed. "It is."

"I was thinking about the tag. Maybe Pops makes Happy sign some kind of contract. In case he burns down the candy store."

"Callback to the Mexican restaurant fire in Scene I."

"Exactly." It was as if we spoke the same code.

He smiled back at me. "I can't wait for Mike to see it," he said. He was like a kid with a new toy. He couldn't wait to show it off.

I looked at my watch. "Peggy gets in at what, nine? We'll be done here in an hour, tops."

He nodded. "I never had it be like this. So easy and good." He leaned back in the armchair and lit a cigarette.

I laughed; it sounded like he was talking about sex. "It sounds like you're talking about sex."

And there he was, blushing again.

"I'm sorry," I said, but it didn't help much. We drank our coffee and puffed on our cigarettes. I cursed myself for opening my big mouth.

Then he said, "Maybe we shouldn't rush it. Sometimes the faster you give them something, the less they think it's worth."

"Hey," I said, leaning forward and forcing him to look me in the eye. "This is good. What we wrote is good."

"You think?"

"I do. And I think we should give it to Mike as soon as possible."

We drove to the studio together; apparently he'd left his car at some bar. We pulled into the parking lot just as Reek was getting out of a beige Mercedes. "Well, aren't you two quite the couple." He arched an eyebrow, looking back and forth between us. Bud was squirming.

I said, "Give us a break, Reek, it's been a long night."

"Are you bragging or complaining?"

Peggy pulled the same shit; when I gave her the rough draft, she said, "Gee, Emmaline, I love your outfit." She knew damned well they were the same clothes I'd worn yesterday. She wiggled her unplucked eyebrows up and down like yo-yos.

I said, "Thank you," as haughtily as I could. It was almost a joke, people thinking Bud and I had slept together. They were missing the whole point. Honestly, fucking someone is simple; it's writing together that's a big deal.

CHAPTER 22 ◆ IF IT WALKS LIKE A MOGUL AND TALKS LIKE A MOGUL ◆

I couldn't believe it. Any of it. I felt *great*. Top of the world didn't even begin to touch it.

We went upstairs, Em and me, and we walked right up to that girl, Peggy. Gave her the script and said, "Could you type this up, please? Right away?" And the cherry on top of the whole thing? Marvin Rudankowitz came lumbering into the office just in time to hear it. "Good morning, Marvin," I said. "Great day, isn't it?"

He froze. Stood there staring at the script in the girl's hand. He looked stupefied, for pete's sake. He didn't think I could do it. Plus which, he looked jealous, too. That look on his face paid me back for sixteen years of never getting a story approved. Of never once feeling like a writer. This morning I did. And it felt *great*.

"What do you want to do now?" Em asked. We were in our office and she was looking at some messages on her desk.

"Celebrate. How about breakfast? My treat."

"Off the lot?"

"Definitely off the lot." I'd have to think of someplace special. Maybe the Biltmore downtown. We could have those champagne and orange juice things. Mimosas.

"Terrific. I just want to do one thing first. Can you wait half a second?"

"I can wait a whole second. That's how good I feel."

She smiled. "Great. I'll be right back."

I followed her back out of our office. The main part of the second floor is open, where the secretaries sit.

The writers' offices, and Mike's and Mel's offices, they all come off that open area. The coffee machine's out there, and the trades are left out there, it's a natural place for people to mill around in. Nobody but me was milling much though. I wandered over to Peggy's desk. "How's it going?" I said.

"Just fine." She didn't even stop typing to say it.

"Wow, you're fast. How long you think it'll take?"

She shrugged. She could do that without stopping, too. "An hour? Hour and a half. You want a hard copy?"

"What does that mean?"

"Paper. You want me to print it up?"

"Yeah." How else would we read it? "And one for Mike, too, okay?" She nodded and kept typing.

I stood around for a while. Nyles Peterson wasn't in yet, I checked. Then I heard Mike coming up the stairs. Naturally, it was easy to tell it was him. For one thing, he makes a lot of noise. His feet kind of *thump* when he walks. He wears these big old sneakers and the way he moves his legs is they sort of come up and almost swing around and down into the ground. More of a *thwack* than a *thump*.

He came into sight around the corner. *Thwacking* and *thumping*. He had his briefcase in one hand and the other arm hung free, both of them twisting forward and back as he lurch-walked. The top of his body, his shoulders mostly, swung in a completely different rhythm than his feet. Thwack right foot, twist right shoulder, thwack left foot, jerk left shoulder. Every other step his briefcase'd bang against his knee. I never thought about it before, but he must be covered in bruises.

"Mike, how you doin'? Great morning, isn't it?"

His face bent up in a grin. "A-nuth-errr shi-dey daay innn pair of dice."

Peggy'd stopped typing. Maybe to catch what Mike was saying. "Another shitty day in paradise," I repeated. "Yeah."

"Good morning, Mr. Lanetti," Peggy said.

"G'dmawn," he said, keeping on course for his office door.

"I feel great," I said to him, walking alongside. "Want to know why? I have really good news. Should I tell you now or should I save it for a surprise later?"

We were at his secretary's desk. She was waving some pink phone message slips.

"The network called twice," she said. "And Monty Newman's manager messengered over this." She held out a white legal-sized envelope which Mike grabbed with his left hand. His fingers seem extra large, maybe because they're always sort of stiff. He clenched them around the envelope and it crumpled in his hand.

Mike went in to his office. I wasn't sure what to do until he said, "Cah-minn." I went in. He flung his briefcase on the desk, moving his arm up over the surface and then opening his fist so the briefcase dropped onto it, then he did the same thing with the envelope and phone messages in his other hand. He turned back toward me. "Shuu-uut thuh doooor."

I did. "What's up?"

I should've sat down, it might've helped. Because what he said next was, "I hear you two are fucking on my time."

Crap. The man ain't a mogul for nothing.

CHAPTER 23 ◆ VIVA ZAPATA ◆

I headed right down to Reek's office. Bud was in a fantastic mood, better than I'd ever seen him, and I wasn't about to let Reek or anyone else spoil it by dumping innuendoes all over him.

I walked across the lobby; his door was closed. I knocked.

"Who is it?"

"Me," I said, opening it wide. He was standing in the middle of the room, throwing eight-by-ten glossies on the floor. He didn't look up. "Reek, I have a bone to pick with you."

He kept tossing pictures. "One minute."

"He's classifying." It was Sahndra, the receptionist. She was standing off to one side.

"Classifying what?" I asked her.

"Actors," she said. "Shhh. You'll disturb his concentration."

The tossing, which I'd assumed was random, turned out to be organized. There were three piles: the first was huge, the second a small mound, and the third contained only a couple of photos. Reek had excellent aim. "Looks like fun," I said.

Sahndra nodded eagerly. "It is. And I'm helping." She was so excited she forgot to whisper.

"Okay, that's it." Reek threw the last picture into the largest pile. He pointed at each as he named it. "*Throwaways, To-be-fileds* and *Callbacks*," he declared.

"How do you tell who goes where?" I asked.

106

"I look at them," he answered, insulted.

"And what do you see?" I was curious.

"Star quality. If it's there. Which it usually isn't."

"He's teaching me to see it, too," Sahndra piped in. She was scooping up the pictures from the throwaway pile and dumping them in the trash. "Mr. Lanetti says if I do a good job and Enrique likes me, I can be his permanent casting assistant."

"You sure that's good news?" I said. Reek glared at me.

"Anything's better than sitting at that desk," she said. "Everyone ogles me."

"I wonder why," said Reek dryly. Sahndra was wearing an impossibly short skirt; as she climbed into the trash can to stomp it down and make room for more photos, we got a great view of her yellow bikini pants. "Here, take these." He handed her the other, considerably smaller piles of photos. "Telephone the callbacks and file the to-be-fileds."

Sahndra nodded. "Got it."

"And close the door after you."

"Okay."

"And kiss the ground three times for Uncle Reek," I said. He didn't laugh, but Sahndra did. He gave her a dirty look and she left.

As soon as the door was shut, he said, "Emmaline, people will never respect you if you're too familiar with them."

"That's what my mother always said. Speaking of which."

"Yes?"

"It's all over the lot that Bud and I are sleeping together." That was an exaggeration, but I thought it was good for effect.

"Is that my fault?" he said.

"I think so. When you're the prick who's spreading the rumors."

He suddenly got very haughty. "I do *not* spread rumors!" he said. "*Ever*! I do *not* gossip! And I *never* tell lies! *My word is my bond!*" His eyes were flashing and his cheeks were blazing; or maybe his eyes were blazing and his cheeks were flashing.

"Calm down. You look like Zorro having PMS."

"When you insult the honor of an Hispanic, you insult his soul. You have no foundation . . ."

"No foundation? You're Information Central around here." Then I took a breath. "Okay, maybe you haven't said anything to anyone yet . . ."

"*Yet*? First you accuse me and now you admit . . ."

"Look, Reek, I personally couldn't give a shit, but it embarrasses Bud. The man hears a sexual reference and he turns the color of tomatoes."

"Then maybe you should be more discreet."

"We have nothing to be discreet *about*. We worked late, that's all."

"Late?"

"All night, as a matter of fact."

"Whatever you say, Emmaline." I shook my head and gave up. I was turning to go when he said, "There is one thing that bothers me. And it's not about you and Bud—whether or not you engage in sordid escapades is of absolutely no interest to me."

"What then?"

He leaned forward and lowered his voice, even though we were alone. "Doesn't it seem strange to you that Michael hasn't got me doing any casting?"

"What's all this?" I gestured at the pictures, the SAG books open on the table.

"This is nothing, this is for extras. I'm talking about the lead. The *star*."

"We just finished the script this morning." I hadn't meant to tell him, and as soon as I did, I was sorry.

His eyebrows arched. "And?"

"And we'll look it over and turn it in to Mike as soon as it's done." He pursed his lips together and regarded me, his eyes dark. "And then Mike will undoubtedly have you start casting."

"Possibly."

"What do you mean, possibly?"

"I mean, possibly this is an exercise in extreme bullshit. Michael never waits for details like a script if he's planning a worldwide talent search."

I was starting to get a headache. "I don't understand. What do you mean, an exercise in bullshit?"

"Did I say *bullshit*? Never mind."

I left. I needed to be out of there. "Goodbye, Reek."

"Write funny!" he said as I shut the door.

CHAPTER 24 ◆ ALONE AT LAST ◆

Em dropped me off at the Blarney Stone in Burbank. There was the new car, right where I'd left it. I don't know if Em was surprised I changed my mind about going to breakfast. She didn't say anything. I didn't say anything either, I just wanted to go home. Try to think.

Mike had made the whole thing seem like a joke. The thing with Em, I mean. As if it was downright hilarious to think she'd be interested in me. Not that I was interested in her. But that was what he thought was funny, the idea that she'd be interested in me. And I couldn't blame him.

It was the cleaning lady's day at Nothing Manors. I threw my jacket on the couch. That helped a little. At least it looked like someone lived there.

Why would Em be interested in me? Why would anyone?

Isabelle was. In Harry's office.

Naw. That was . . . well, I don't know what that was.

It was her coming on to you. Would you like to see what you missed, that's what she said. What else could she mean?

I don't know and it doesn't matter. Nothing's going to happen.

It might if you call her. That's the ticket, Goodman, call her up. If Harry answers, you give him some crap about the car. But if it's her, if it's Isabelle, you say, Yeah, I definitely want to see what I missed. And you tell her all about how you feel.

How I feel. That's a good one.

I loved Isabelle the first time I saw her. I loved her the whole time we were living together, even though there was nothing in it, I mean, nothing like a real marriage in it. We never, you know, had sex or anything. That probably sounds crazy, I mean, I know it sounds crazy. But we used to sit in the kitchen. Drinking coffee, talking. We'd sit there till two, three in the morning. Just talking. Then the phone'd ring and off she'd go. To Harry. Dumpy shlumpy goddam rich Harry. I can't even remember most people's names, but I can close my eyes and remember what Isabelle was wearing every single time I saw her.

So what do you think? Should I tell her all that?

I don't know, Goodman. I'd edit.

I went in the bathroom, I figured I'd shower. Maybe watch some TV. Only while I was standing there I got one of those accidental glimpses of myself. In the medicine cabinet mirror. Those accidental glimpses are murder.

It's not like I spend a lot of time looking at myself. I mean, why would I, right? Now that I did, hell, I barely recognized myself. I looked saggy and I had pouches where I didn't used to have pouches. Things were in different places, hair was in different places. It was like you had to keep tabs on your face all the time. While you weren't looking, it could change into someone else's.

Why would Isabelle be interested in that? Or Emmaline, for that matter? When it got right down to it, I wasn't even interested.

CHAPTER 25 ◆ TAKE ME TO YOUR MOGUL, PLEASE ◆

Bud and I turned the script in to Mike, and that was it, we were back to the waiting mode. There was no telling when we'd hear; if you're the Mogul, you can take all the time you want.

On Friday, we ate lunch out on the patio. Reek had invited himself to join us, and he was bitching. "I don't know why we have to eat out here," he said, waving away flies.

"No one told you to bring your family," Bud said.

I laughed, but Reek glowered. "There's a perfectly good executive dining room inside," he said. He was right; there *was* a private dining room, complete with waitresses and white tablecloths. Originally, it was so the executives could avoid the masses, but now anyone with $8.95 for a tuna melt could eat there.

"The executive dining room," I said, "is full of schmucks."

Bud nodded. "We oughta know. We ate in there yesterday."

"At least it's clean." Reek rubbed at a sticky spot on the table like it was a tubercular stain.

"You just like to be waited on," I said to him.

"Yes, I do. Why not?"

"At least you're honest." I lit a cigarette and pushed the pack toward Bud, who'd left his in the office again.

"Thanks." Bud took a Marlboro.

"You two are starting to act married," Reek said.

I looked at Bud; I wanted to make sure this was treated as a joke. I said, "Honey, I'm home."

Reek pouted. "Go ahead, make fun. But you two have produced something more important than children: you gave birth to a script."

Bud exhaled smoke. "I'm too young to be a father," he said.

Just then, a limousine pulled up. Hardly anyone drives through that alley. The car, long and black, came right up to the patio and stopped; the uniformed driver got out and opened the back door. A beat-up white sneaker emerged. It was Mike. "Fucking A," I said.

"Shh," Reek hissed, so low I could barely hear him.

Two men in suits climbed out of the limo behind Mike. "Who are they?" I asked.

Reek barely moved his lips. "The one on the left is Adrian Fuller. President of the network. The other one's Ed Cooper. Veep in charge of west coast production."

Mike, as usual, looked as precarious as one of those round-bottomed punching bags. He tottered toward us, grinning like crazy. The other people on the patio were staring. Clearly loving the attention, he called up to us, "I've been tap dancing for the big boys."

"Yeah, but *you* have to wear the taps on your knees," Bud yelled back.

Mike burst out with that barking, braying laugh; his face would freeze, the muscles around his mouth pulled taut. Adrian Fuller and his buddy watched him and chuckled nervously. "I wanted them to meet you," the Mogul said. His arm jerked toward us. "Bud Goodman and Emmaline Goldman Grosvenor." It took him forever to say my name: *Emm-uhh-li-iiine.* If it were anyone else, I would've thought he was being sarcastic.

We shook hands over the railing and there was an awkward silence. I realized Reek hadn't been introduced. "You know Enrique Carlos?"

"Of course," said Reek. "Nice to see you again, gentlemen."

Mike seemed to grimace. I wondered how long you had to know him to figure out what those twitches and spasms meant. Looking at Bud, he said, "I need to see you two. Give me an hour."

This is it, I thought. Keep your mouth shut, I heard Reek's voice say in my head. I did. The three men left through the alley, Mike staggering in the middle, and the executives each giving him a wide berth.

"There goes pure power," Reek whispered, awe in his voice. "The president of the network."

"What's with that white hair?" I said. "He looks like a Q-tip."

Reek sighed. "Emmaline, you are hopeless."

"Thanks, Reek. What do you think they're meeting about?"

He considered. "If I had to make a guess, I'd say it's probably about that script you two wrote."

I glanced at Bud, then back at Reek. "Have you heard something?"

"*Heard something*? Does that mean you think I'm incapable of forming my own opinion?"

"Christ, Reek, you get insulted more easily than anyone I have ever met."

"That's right, why should I get insulted?" He threw his hands up in the air. "Just because you sit here calling me *Reek*, and Michael fails to introduce me at all, and no one even considers the possibility of making this new character ethnic. What kind of name is *Happy* anyway?"

"Wait a minute," I said. "You read the script?"

He ignored me. "*Happy, Lucky.* Who named these people, the Seven Dwarves?"

Bud looked up. "Good idea for a guest shot."

"Enrique," I said again, "did you read the script?"

"Did I say I did?" he asked.

I sighed. "I thought there was some crucial protocol about Michael reading everything first."

"The point is, if I don't think about casting minorities, who will?"

"That's not the point. The point is, do you know anything about Mike's reaction, or the network's reaction to the script?"

"Wheels within wheels, Emmaline."

"Which means what?" As usual when I spoke with Reek, I was getting a headache.

"I can't say any more." Solemnly, he stood up.

After he left, I turned to Bud. "Do you have any idea what he just said?"

Bud sighed heavily. "No. But I guess it's time to find out." Looking like a condemned man who didn't even get his last meal, he pushed himself away from the table.

CHAPTER 26 ◆ WHO KNOWS? ◆

Mike was on the phone when we got to his office. "So you got the roses," he said to whoever he was talking to. He waved at us to sit down. I guess that's what he meant by flapping his arm at the furniture.

Em had just plopped down on one of the couches when Katrina Rhinestone stuck her head in. "Harris and Weiner on line two," she said.

"For me?" Em said.

"No," said Katrina, "for Mr. Lanetti."

Em said, "Sorry." Then she looked at me and shrugged. "I'm with Harris and Weiner, too."

She had the same agent as Mike? Maybe that's how she got the job.

"Why not a hundred?" Mike was saying into the phone. "I like the number. It's nice and round." Then he laughed that maniac laugh of his. The one that sounds like a cross between a donkey and I don't know what. Maybe another donkey.

He finally finished and hung up. He banged the receiver down, then had to move it into place with his hand. It took a minute for him to get it right. His fingers don't bend too well for one thing.

"Another one of your flames?" I said, pointing to the phone.

I knew he'd like that. "Jacgk-ah-leen," he grinned. "Bisset."

"You sent Jacqueline Bisset a hundred roses?" Em was impressed.

"A hundred rose *bushes*." Mike laughed like it was some big joke and his head bobbed around. But then he was ready to talk. He said, "We're back in the shit."

I said, "I didn't know we ever got out of it."

He laughed. He was in a great mood for laughing today. He said, "Monty's not coming back."

"That what you were talking to the brass about?" I asked.

He shrugged, I think. "Among other things," he said.

Em looked confused. "I thought we knew Monty was out."

Mike said, "Yeah, but now we know it's true."

"Have you talked to him?" Me. I was curious.

"Negotiations have broken down." Mogul talk. Then he got serious. "Listen, I want you two to read something." He fumbled around in a briefcase on the floor, finally lifting it up onto his desk.

"Can I help?" Em asked, standing up.

"Yes." He flopped back in his chair. "Take those out."

She pulled out two scripts with bright orange covers. "These?" He nodded and waved his arm at me. Em handed me a script. It read, "*Bigelow's Boys. Twenty Seconds Over Tokyo.*" No writer's credit.

"Catchy title," I said.

"It's the best thing about it, believe me." He watched us thumb through it. At least, Em was thumbing through it. "I'd like your thoughts on it."

"Okay," I said, starting to get up.

"Wait a minute." That was Em, of course. "What about our script?" she said.

"What script?" he asked.

"The new show. We turned it in . . ." She looked over at me. "Tuesday?" I nodded. "Tuesday," she said back at him.

He jerked in his chair. A spasm, I guess. He said, "Oh yeah. Soon. Tomorrow. We'll talk." He was done.

Em didn't get that Mike was done. "Okay," I said, standing up and looking at her. "Let's get out before he calls another movie star." I leaned over and pulled her up by the arm. "Really. Next on his list is Madonna. My ears aren't mature enough for that."

Mike yukked it up and Em let me lead her out. "See you later," she called to Mike. As soon as we were clear of his secretary's desk, Em said, "What was all that about?"

"I don't know." But I know better than to tell a mogul what to do.

"You do, too. You know something."

She followed me into our office and shut the door. I didn't know anything, not for sure, but I knew it didn't look good. The new show was either still up in the air or out of the picture completely. Why else would he give us *Bigelow's Boys*? All that good writing we did. All for zip.

"Bud?"

You've got to tell her, Goodman. You owe her that much.

"Okay, but let's go someplace."

She looked confused. "I don't understand . . ."

"Come on," I said. "We have to talk."

CHAPTER 27 ◆ YOU THINK I ACT THIS WAY ON PURPOSE? ◆

Bud took me to a place called Phillipe's. It was in a downtown neighborhood that looked like it had never heard of Hollywood. The buildings were old, two-storied, and adorned with plaster curlicues. Bud parked on a hill. I kept quiet; he hates to talk while he's parking.

Inside, Phillipe's belonged to another time zone. There was sawdust on the floor and long wooden tables were surrounded by mismatched chairs and stools. A few people sat scattered around, an old man in an overcoat, a business-type with a newspaper. Across the room from us was another entrance, and next to that door was an old brass scale. A wooden display case held candy, gum, cigars, cigarettes; it was enclosed in a filigreed wire cage and had a sign over it that said *Cashier*. A woman about sixty with dyed black hair sat on a stool, smoking and reading a paperback.

We walked down some steps and up to a glass and chrome case that held the food: cheesecakes, pies, salads, pickles, slabs of meats, hunks of cheese. Bud and I got in a line that said *Beer Only*. The menu was on the wall, one of those black felt boards you stick the little white letters into. There was also a profusion of hand-painted signs: *Coffee Refill Still Only Five Cents, Ice-Cold Lemonade, Ask About Our Cream Pies, Lamb Dip,* and *French Dip Our Specialty.*

"Next." It was our turn. We faced a red-haired woman dressed in white; her nametag said *Arlene*.

"What kind of beer you want?" Bud asked me.

A shelf on the back wall displayed several imported beer bottles. I was about to order a Heineken when I noticed a neon clock that said *This Bud's For You*. I laughed and said, "I'll have a Bud."

He gave me a look, then turned back to Arlene. "Two Buds. And two pickled eggs, please."

"This is supposed to be a Beer Only line," said Arlene.

"Oh, I thought it said *Beer Lonely*. That's why I figured we oughta get it a couple of pickled eggs."

"I remember you," she said, shooting him one of those motherly-affection-but-I-don't-approve looks. Then she went and got two fuchsia eggs out of a huge jar.

Bud picked up the tray Arlene had loaded and found a wooden booth in the corner. "How do you know about this place?" I asked.

He shrugged. "It used to be better. They redid it all."

Sometimes he was like an old man, I thought. The beer was ice-cold and tasted great. "So, what are those purple eggs like?"

"Here." He held out the plate and I picked one up and took a bite. It was awful. I had to drink some beer to get it down. "They make them with beets," he said.

"I can tell. I hate beets."

"Oh." He munched his egg. I sipped my beer. I felt awkward, and I usually feel so comfortable with Bud. Then he said, "Listen, Em, about in Mike's office." I nodded, but he hesitated and lit a cigarette so he wouldn't have to talk. Finally, he said, "I don't think it has anything to do with us, it's all mogul moves. But you can't push Mike into a corner, you can't try and tell him what to do."

"I wasn't trying to." All I wanted was for Mike to read our script. "Do you think Mike thought I was telling him what to do?"

"Well . . ." Bud shrugged, then sighed. "I don't know. Who can tell what Mike's thinking?"

"Shit." I was always doing the wrong thing lately. "I'm sorry."

"It's no big deal, it's just . . ." He stopped. I couldn't tell if he didn't know what to say or he was afraid to say it.

"What?"

"Well, our script. I think we did a good job, I'm not saying it has anything to do with that, but . . ." He took a breath and finished. "I think Mike's planning to eat it."

What did that mean? "Eat it?"

"Dump it. Shelve it. Bury it."

"Okay," I said, "I get it. Why?"

He shrugged. "Who knows? They're obviously still negotiating with Monty Newman. Maybe Mike wanted the script for leverage. There could be a million things going on behind the scenes that you and I don't get and never will."

"Wheels within wheels," I said. "You think Enrique knows something?"

"I guess there's a slim possibility."

"What a bunch of shit." Would he really dump our script?

"And another thing," Bud asked. "You're with Harris and Weiner?"

"Yeah. Ken Harris." I always thought he sounded like an actor.

"So is Mike."

"Mike's with Brad Weiner. An agent named Weiner seems redundant, don't you think?"

He ignored that. "Is your deal with *Life With Lucky* or Lanetti Enterprises?"

"I have no idea."

"Be good to find out," he said.

"Okay." He was playing with his empty glass. "I'll get this round." I got two more beers and a bag of chips. Bud was smoking when I came back, and the egg I'd taken the bite out of was still on the plate.

We both poured beer into our glasses.

I couldn't help myself "Don't you find this pretty fucking ironic? Here we are, toiling away at the business of communicating, neither one of us knows anything that's going on, and we work for a guy whose words are barely understandable, much less his motives. I call it pretty fucking ironic."

Bud nodded, took a swig of beer. He said, "Is that what you think we do? Toil away at, you know, communicating?"

"I guess. Don't you?" He just looked at me. "Not that it's actually possible."

He frowned. "What do you mean?"

"Communicating. I mean, don't you ever feel inadequate when you're trying to explain something important?"

"I've made feeling inadequate a way of life," he said. He was in his hunched-over position, shoulders protecting his beer. Shit, maybe I should just shut up. "What do you mean, you don't think it's possible?"

"I just don't know if we can ever achieve any real degree of *understanding*." He looked at me blankly. I said, "Obviously, I can make you understand this is a bag of potato chips and that's a bottle of beer, but Christ, anything deeper than that, or anything more abstract..." Was I making any sense? "The trouble is, if I'm going to explain to you how I'm feeling, first I have to understand it myself. Then when you add in the sexual component..."

"What sexual component?"

"Shit—men, women." What was I saying? Did I honestly believe communication was impossible? Why the fuck did I become a writer? I said, "I guess the challenge is to try."

We sat there. It was hard not to feel glum. I know I felt glum, and Bud looked like the physical embodiment of glum. Eventually, we both got lamb dip sandwiches, which were wonderful, especially with the mustard they had out on the table. *Hot, but good,* it said on the jar.

"Maybe the next mogul moves will be to our advantage," I said hopefully.

Bud shook his head. "Mogul moves are never to anyone's advantage but the mogul."

CHAPTER 28 ◆ WHAT AM I DOING? ◆

We were sitting at the traffic light at the bottom of the hill. I was going to drop her off back at the studio. She said, "What's that building?" Pointing across the street.

"Union Station," I said.

"The train station?"

"Yeah." She'd never been there but she said it looked familiar. "Probably because of old movies," I said.

"The Postman Always Rings Twice. When John Garfield drops off Lana Turner."

"Uh huh." That was a great scene. He picked up a redhead right in the parking lot.

"What about *Double Indemnity*?"

"That was Glendale," I told her. "Or maybe a set." Then I had a thought. "You want to go inside?"

"Could we?" She looked excited.

The fact of the matter is, Union Station's one of my favorite places in L.A. For starters, it's huge. Big open rooms and long wide corridors. The floors are marble, mostly jasper that was quarried right in California. When you walk, your footsteps echo. It's like being in a church.

We parked the car and I gave her the tour, the whole nine yards with the murals on the ceilings and the old wooden ticket booths. We were walking down the hallway with the long rows of leather armchairs. Em said, "I keep expecting to see Carole Lombard come around the corner."

"You really like old movies?" I was surprised.

"I love old movies. Thanks for showing me this place."

"Yeah. No problem."

"What's out there?" She pointed to an exit.

"A courtyard. We can get out that way."

It was dark outside and the courtyard was empty. There were square planters made out of painted Mexican tiles and filled with palm trees and wavy-edged elephant ears. Green spotlights were camou-flaged in the fronds. Standing out there, the smell of jasmine was like perfume and you couldn't help breath-ing it in.

She sat down and took out her cigarettes. I always left mine at the office or home, hoping I'd quit, but I always wound up having one of her Marlboros. "I see why you like this place," she said.

"Why?" I wasn't really sure myself.

"It's an anachronism. It's pure Hollywood, but only the good, beautiful part. None of the ugliness and shit. It's romantic."

I didn't know what to say.

"Don't you believe in romantic love?"

I said, "I believe in rheumatic love."

"What's that mean?"

"Love is sick." Ba dump bump.

"You make a lousy cynic, Bud." She was smiling.

When I sat down next to her I could see the moon just up over the edge of the rounded clay tiles on the roof. I liked the way the tiles fit together, a row of them curved outward fitting into a row curved in. I said, "You remember when you were talking before. About communicating and understanding between, you know, men and women?"

"Uh huh."

"I think our script proves it's possible. To communicate. We did it."

"That's a really nice thing to say, Bud. A really positive thing."

I'd wanted to say it. I'd forced myself to say it, not to think it all out beforehand. I was glad now. I felt bad before, having to tell her about the script and Mike. Now I felt like putting my arm around her. Telling her jokes. Making her laugh.

Going to bed with her.

She said, "Bud, are you okay?"

"Huh?"

"You look terrible. Awful."

"You think plastic surgery'd help?"

She laughed, thank God. I needed time. I couldn't believe I was thinking about what I was thinking about.

CHAPTER 29 ◆ IT'S ALL IN THE TIMING ◆

Bud was planning to drive me back to the studio, but I suggested going to my place. He didn't exactly jump at the idea.

"I've been talking too much, haven't I?"

He shook his head, "No, it's just, you know . . ." He trailed off, gripping both hands tightly on the steering wheel. Then he said, "I just don't want you to think I have the wrong idea about going back to your place."

"What wrong idea? Oh, shit." Was I supposed to be afraid he was thinking unclean thoughts about me? "Bud, you are unbelievably corny."

"Yeah. When I die, they'll use me for niblets."

"Look, it just feels nice to be out. To talk. No big deal."

"Okay." He nodded, started the car and we drove to my house. Naturally, once we were there, I was completely self-conscious, so I rolled a joint.

"You want some?" I asked. Bud was on the couch; I was on the rug.

"Thanks, I'll stick to this." He was drinking Baileys Irish Cream. I didn't even know I had any until he had pulled the bottle out of the cupboard. He looked around the room, at books, paintings, every object but me. I was trying to figure out why he seemed different. He looked less pudgy than usual, less like the Pillsbury Doughboy. He was wearing a blue sweater, over a blue shirt, and they made his blue eyes even bluer.

This was silly. I was horny, that's all. It was over three years since Ned left. I hadn't slept with anyone I liked in a long time.

I looked at Bud, sitting on the couch like a round-shouldered lump. I'd never get him to make a move. Then he cleared his throat. I thought, wouldn't it be astonishing if he were thinking the same thing I was?

He said, "You mind if I move these pillows?"

"Throw them out the fucking window, I don't care." I flipped the joint into the ashtray.

"Maybe I should go," he said.

"No. I'm sorry. I'm just feeling a little weird." Like I'm suddenly attracted to you and I don't know why but I think it's probably a horrible idea anyway. "You want a cigarette?"

"Yeah, okay."

"How about a movie?" I said. "I have lots of tapes."

Of course, he loved movies. We stood in front of the bookcase reading titles together. He was so solid standing there. I thought, if I could just lean against him . . .

"You have *Sunset Boulevard*," he said, pulling out the cassette. "Not many movies start out with a dead narrator."

"A dead *writer* narrator."

He got a funny expression on his face and then quoted, "As long as the lady's buying, why not just *feel* the vicuña?"

"I think it needs to be rewound," I said. I put the tape in the VCR and pushed the rewind button. Bud was pacing around the room.

It's a shame mind reading isn't possible. Bud often talked about it, asking me if I believed in it. The tape was almost done. I started concentrating.

Do you wanna fuck? Do you wanna fuck?

I thought it best to be direct. I was expecting a miracle, after all, so it seemed a good idea to keep it simple.

Do you wanna fuck? Do you wanna fuck?

He stopped moving around and stared at me. I did it! He cleared his throat.

"Yes?" I said eagerly.

"Can I use your bathroom?"

"Sure." He turned; in a minute he'd be gone. "Bud?"

"Yeah?" He stopped in the doorway, just like I knew he would.

"Do you want to . . . stay over?" I couldn't believe I, of all people, was using a euphemism. Then I saw him look at the couch; he didn't even understand. I said, "You know, when you said before you didn't want me to think you were coming over for the wrong reason. Would you like to? Be here for the wrong reason?"

"Huh?"

Oh, Christ. "Bud, do you wanna fuck?"

He gulped. "Can I go to the bathroom first?"

Shit. How humiliating was this?

"I would . . . you know . . ."

"What?"

"Like to . . . do it."

Oh, Jesus. "Do it?" I almost laughed.

He shrugged. "You know."

"You couldn't want to too badly. Not if you have to run and hide in the bathroom first."

"I wasn't going to hide. And I'm sorry if I don't know the etiquette." There was something in his tone, something new, almost bold.

"No," I said, "my fault. I should've, I mean, I shouldn't have said anything."

"You just surprised me," he said.

This is the most excruciatingly embarrassing moment of my life, I thought. "I know. I'm sorry."

"It wasn't the bad kind of surprise . . ."

I looked at him. His face seemed so open, and his eyes, instead of darting around the room or studying his fingernails, were staring right back at me. If this were a movie, I thought, we'd walk to each other and kiss. Neither one of us moved. The VCR made a loud click.

"I think the tape's rewound," he said.

He moved to the couch. I picked up the remote and we both sat gingerly. "Great opening credits," he said. Big white block letters appeared against the pavement of what was supposed to be Sunset Boulevard. It looked like Sunset Boulevard. For all I knew, it was Kalama-fucking-zoo.

Then Bud's hand brushed the outside of my thigh. I shifted, not away, just to move. There was no response. It must've been an accident, I thought.

We watched the opening, with poor William Holden floating face down; we both laughed at the line about always wanting a pool. I leaned down to get my cigarettes off the coffee table. "Want one?" I whispered. Bud murmured yes, and I lit them both from the same match.

I settled back on the couch a little closer to him. Testing. It was the scene where William Holden goes to pick up his car from the shoeshine guy. There's a line: "He never had to ask how you were doing—he'd just look at your heels and know." I felt a distinct pressure against my leg. I pressed back. The TV seemed very loud. I think it was because neither one of us was breathing.

I don't know who moved. It must've been Bud; I don't think it was me. But suddenly we were kissing. What a surprise. And not the bad kind of surprise either.

CHAPTER 30 ◆ I WANT TO, I WANT TO! ◆

I learned how to kiss with Linda, my first wife. For six years that's all we did. She never even let me touch her breast until we were practically married. Even then I'd only get to touch the right one. I don't know why. I never had the nerve to ask her. I was afraid she'd change her mind about the right one, too.

The room was swaying. Maybe it was the booze. But when I put my hand on Em's blouse, I never felt anything so soft in my life. I started unbuttoning it. She watched me. Let me. When I got it open, she was wearing a black lace bra. I went for the right one. Out of habit.

"Bud?"

Uh oh. I knew things were going too good.

She said, "There's one thing I'm worried about."

"Oh yeah. I was tested after my last, you know, experience." I didn't have to tell her that was after Joyce and nearly two years ago, did I?

She smiled. "Good, but I was thinking about our writing together."

She was thinking about that now? "Yeah?"

"I just don't want to fuck that up."

How bad did she think I was? "Do you want to stop?" I hated myself as soon as I said it.

She didn't say anything for a minute. Then, "I suppose it could make things even better." She slid her hand down to unzip my fly.

"Unnnngh."

"You think that's possible? Bud?"

"Oh yeah . . ."

"As long as we're careful, right?"

"Yeah, careful. Right." Right, left, right, left. Kiss one, then the other.

"It could make our friendship that much deeper."

"Deeper . . ." Oh God, Emmaline.

Then it happened. I opened my eyes. She opened hers. We looked at each other. And neither one of us said a word.

129

Maybe that doesn't sound like much. Maybe it wouldn't be much to anyone else. But for that one second, which lasted at least a million years, we connected. We communicated. I felt like yelling. Only I didn't have to, she already knew.

After a while, we got up and went to her bedroom. I'm too old to be wrestling around on bad sofa springs. We hardly said a word the rest of the night. Sounds mostly, a few syllables. But that feeling of connecting, it stayed.

Later—afterwards—I looked at her before I turned out the light. One small curl was stuck to her cheek. Her mouth was open. She looked wonderful.

You're falling in love, Goodman.

I know. And I thought *she* was crazy.

I woke up feeling great. None of that where am I crap, either. I remembered right away I was at Em's. I remembered everything.

The thing of it is, maybe feeling great can't last. Like those ice sculptures they always have at weddings. Some guy worked like crazy making that swan out of ice. But the second it's finished, it starts to melt.

I wasn't going to let that happen. I thought, I'll roll over and see Em. And that'll make me feel even greater. So I did it, I rolled over.

She wasn't there. Right away, the swan's starting to melt.

Then I got this idea. Em's pillow was there. And like those perfume ads where they talk about how the scent lingers, I'd smell her lingering scent.

Goodman, the only scent around here suggests you need a shower. What if she comes in and catches you?

She'll think I'm being corny again.

Corny is one thing, psychotic's another. Look at that pillow: there's nothing on it but her mascara and your nose hairs.

I got out of bed. It was filled with melted ice anyway. I went looking for Em. The bathroom door was closed. I said, "You in there?" Before she could answer me, the phone rang. "I'll get it." I didn't even stop to think she might not want me answering her phone.

It was Katrina. Mike's secretary. She said, "Bud?" It was a question but it wasn't. She knew it was me.

"Yeah, this is Bud." I had nothing to hide.

She said, "I'm looking for Emmaline Grosvenor. Mr. Lanetti would like to see the two of you at the studio at 11:00. This is curious, Bud, because I tried to reach you earlier at the number I have on my staff list and there was no answer. I then called the number I have listed for Emmaline Grosvenor and got you. Is it possible there's a typo?"

I said, "Did you say 11:00?"

"Yes, I did." Her voice went up at the end. Like she was about to ask another question.

I said, "Okay, thanks. We'll be there."

She said, "Don't forget to tell Emmaline." I'm pretty sure she was laughing when she hung up.

I told Em about Mike wanting to see us again. I had to talk through the bathroom door. I said, "This might be good news. It isn't the usual mogul style. Of course, it might be bad news. But I have this feeling. A good feeling. Fact of the matter is, I woke up with it."

She didn't say anything. "Em, can you say something?"

Nothing.

"Can you hear me?"
More nothing.
I turned the knob. The door opened. "Em?"
The bathroom was empty. She was gone.
See, Goodman? That's what you get for waking up happy.

CHAPTER 31 ◆ DRIVE, SHE SAID ◆

In some cities, people walk. In Los Angeles, people who walk get run over. Unless they're ethnic, then they get arrested. Angelenos don't necessarily *want* to spend their lifetimes in cars; they do it out of self-defense.

I took Bud's keys and drove his car to the studio. There wasn't much traffic. Everyone was home asleep. Bud, for example, was at *my* home asleep.

I picked up my Fiat and took off. I used to do this all the time, get up early and work myself into a Joan Didion-inspired trance. It's therapeutic; you can forget anything while you're driving. The Fiat felt good, responsive, *mine*. I headed west on Sunset, then cut over to cruise through Hancock Park. I like it there, the houses are huge and set way back, with impeccably manicured lawns. You never see any people in Hancock Park.

I made a right on Wilshire. I never drive on Wilshire, there's too much traffic and a signal every fucking block, but this morning the street was mine, not another car in sight. All the lights were green, a long succession of *go* stretching out to infinity. Or at least to Beverly Hills.

I began to relax. I put on an old Kinks CD, lit a joint and rocked and rolled down Wilshire Boulevard in my hot Italian convertible. Then a street sign caught my eye. I was in Westwood already, near where Bud lived. Shit.

I hung a left and headed for the freeway, what I like to call the ditch. The ditch is hard-core, the driving junkie's morphine. It's a conveyor belt moving at sixty miles an hour minimum, and that's in both directions. People are fallible though; people screw up. That station wagon full of illegal aliens could come blasting through the Jersey barrier and crash head-on into me. Wouldn't that be funny?

I should never have slept with Bud. I don't even know why I did. I was drawn in by his warmth, which is unfair. And his humor. And his touch, which was tender and somehow unbelievably *sure*. It was like a gift, making love with Bud, hearing him breathe my name. *Em.* I never had a nickname before.

None of that is the point, however, since it all boils down to this: I have *always* been the one who says *I love you* first, who bares my soul and waits while the schmuck I'm staring at tries to think of something to say back. Just once, I want someone to fall in love with *me*, to pledge eternal devotion to *me*.

I got off the ditch. While I was waiting at a Stop sign, the car coming toward me turned without signaling. Signaling's a sign of weakness in L.A.: never reveal your strategy. I turned off my blinker and made a furtive left.

CHAPTER 32 ◆ THE EARTH MOVED AND NOW I CAN'T FIND A THING ◆

I'd smoked about a pack and a half of cigarettes by the time Em came back. I finished the pack by her bed. Found a new pack in her kitchen.

I guess I was listening for *my* car. That's why I didn't hear her. I was out on the porch but she was inside the door before I had a chance to do anything.

"Hi," I said. Lame.

She was holding a white bag like you get from a bakery. She looked around the room and I looked at her. Then we switched, she looked at me and I looked around the room. We were being, what's the word? Wary.

Then she said, "Did you do that?" She was pointing at this red bucket of sand I was using for an ashtray.

"Yeah."

She said, "This is not an ashtray." And she started plucking out the butts. She put the white bag down so she could use both hands.

I said, "I'm sorry." I tried to help her, but she wouldn't let me. That's when I noticed there was a plaster hand sticking out of the sand. "What is this thing anyway?" I said.

"It's an early piece of Ned's. Called *Revenge of the Sand Castle*." I thought she was joking. I guess I laughed, because she gave me a dirty look. And said, "You obviously know nothing about art."

I said, "I know you're not supposed to use it for an ashtray." She didn't even crack a smile. "Em? I think I know why you left this morning."

"Really?" She wouldn't look at me. Just sat there, smoothing the sand. But I could tell she was listening.

I said, "Yeah. I know what it's like sometimes, how you feel like getting off by yourself. I understand."

"Well then," she said, "it's a good thing I got to the car first."

What the hell's going on here?

Simple, Goodman. You should never have slept with her.

Great. *Now* you tell me.

CHAPTER 33 ◆ IF YOU DON'T CARE, I DON'T CARE ◆

Bud white-knuckled the dashboard as I accelerated into a turn. Depression, I decided, is having all your most paranoid fantasies confirmed. Bud didn't give a shit about last night; he didn't even want to talk about it. He was too busy telling me about why Mike might want to have this meeting.

Keeping my left hand on the steering wheel, I took an onion bagel out of the bag. As I put it in my mouth, I said, "Help yourself." They were my first words since getting in the car; you can't beat sex for bringing people closer.

I pulled into the studio lot and parked in my assigned space; there was Bud's Buick, sitting by itself where I'd left it. "Thanks for letting me take your car this morning. Even though I didn't ask." I guess I was trying to stop being so shitty.

"That's okay," he said, "I prefer not to be asked." Then he got a sheepish look on his face. "Em . . ." he started.

I knew he was going to talk about last night.

"About last night . . ."

There was an alarming shriek of brakes and Mike's Ferrari suddenly skidded up next to us. The woman behind the wheel was young and blonde, wearing lots of makeup and a sequined red dress. Mike was struggling with the door and they were both laughing. "Push!" Mike yelled at her. The girl laughed and pushed him with her bare foot; he flew out of the car, and would've hit the ground if Bud hadn't scrambled to catch him. I need a seat ejector," Mike said, giggling.

The blonde pulled the car door shut and did a U-turn around us. "Don't forget to have it washed!" Mike called, although she was gone long before he finished shouting. We headed for the building, Bud and I walking slowly to match Mike's uneven lurch. He said, "She's a hooker."

I didn't know what to say. "And you trust her with your Ferrari?"

"I trusted her with more than that," Mike leered. "All night long."

When we got upstairs, there was a large carton sitting beside Katrina Rhinestone's desk. "My chair!" Mike bleated.

We helped him slash open the cardboard—I found an Exacto knife in Peggy's desk drawer—and unpack his new chair. "It's called a Sector Command Chair," he announced with glee. He'd special-ordered it from some catalog company on the east coast and it was lushly high tech, a sort of combination armchair–pilot's seat. The solid-cast aluminum frame had five splayed legs, each ending in an oversized black caster. Covered in soft black leather, it smelled like a new car. There were two levers underneath the seat, one for the height control and the other for tilt. It came with a manual that I thumbed through while Bud pushed Mike around the office. Every time we discovered a new feature or doohickey—like the pneumatic lift—it was another fifteen minutes. I lost interest in it long before Mike did, or even Bud.

Eventually, we wheeled him into his office. Bud carried out the old chair while Mike adjusted himself behind his desk. "Do I look like a sector commander?" he asked me with a grin.

"Captain Kirk reborn," I said.

"Up, up and away!" He flipped a lever and the chair tilted dangerously back. I jumped up to help him, but he was laughing uproariously, his feet kicking wildly. He flipped the lever again and the chair gently righted itself "I love new toys!" he said.

Bud came in and sat. "I had a GI Joe I liked a lot."

Mike laughed happily, then clapped his hands together. Sometimes he held them like that, gripped together, I think to keep them under control. "Let's talk about your script."

Maybe we *weren't* getting the Mogul dump. At least Mike had read the script. I was excited, but when Bud spoke, his voice had its typical ho-hum, another-day-in-hell tone. "You go first," he said to Mike.

"I loved it," Mike announced. I felt a lump I didn't even know I had dissolve in my stomach. "The dialogue's good, the character's well-developed. The first act is solid. One of the best first acts I've ever seen."

Bud and I grinned at each other. I wanted to jump up and hug him. I couldn't have written Mike a better speech if I'd tried.

Then he said, "Now, to save time, I thought we'd do the rewrite ourselves."

Bud had warned me that Mike would probably turn the script over to someone else for the rewrite; his guess was Rudankowitz and Pfeiffer, an appalling idea. Mike's suggestion was miles better: we could protect the script and besides, I'd never written with a Mogul. "Terrific," I said.

Mike's chair swiveled toward me. "I meant Bud and me," he said.

"Oh," I managed.

"Only because it'll be faster," the Mogul said. "We've worked together before. Know each other's styles."

Mike started turning pages, and Bud lit a cigarette. I noticed it was a pack of mine. "Okay, then." I stood up. "You guys want the bagels? I'd be glad to leave them."

"Thanks," said Mike.

"Sure." I stood at the door a minute, waiting for Bud to look up. He didn't. He wouldn't.

CHAPTER 34 ◆ CAUGHT BETWEEN A ROCK ◆

I was caught all right. Mike didn't want Em around for the rewrite. And I was right in the middle. Caught between a rock and a hard-on, pardon my language.

After he kicked her out, he said, "The more I think about it, the more I think I ought to let Emmaline go."

I said, "Oh yeah?" I didn't want Mike to think I cared. He might fire Em right off the bat.

"She doesn't have the temperament for our kind of show."

I said, "Is her deal up soon?" Mike hates to pay people off.

He said, "I'm sure we can work it out. She's with Harris and Weiner." So he knew they had the same agent. That's what I was thinking. When Mike said, "All this'd be different if you'd fucked her."

You blew it, Goodman. Never turn your back on a mogul.

I said, "Yeah, well . . . I, you know . . ."

Mike said, "Then you *are* fucking her."

Go on, Goodman, tell him you only did it once.

Twice, really. Okay, once and a half.

Mike waved his hand. Being fatherly. Ben Cartwright talking to Little Joe. Or was I Hoss? He said, "Maybe we can turn this to our advantage."

"Meaning what?"

"I saw the stories she pitched to Mel. They were good."

That surprised me. "You liked them?"

His shoulders jerked up to his ears. I guess he was shrugging. He said, "The point is, Mel passed on them. Because he knew Monty would want him to. That's unfair treatment. Discrimination. Breach of contract." He paused. "If you ask her to do something, will she?"

I thought about this morning. "What do you want her to do?"

"We'll get into the details later." I guess I was stalling because he said, "Go talk to her. The world of art can wait five minutes." He fumbled with the script and I went downstairs.

She was in her car. Crying. She didn't even hear me say her name. I tapped on the window, and she jumped out and started hugging me.

We stayed like that for a while. Then she said, "I'm so glad you came out." I gave her my handkerchief and she blew her nose. "I hate it when I do this." I didn't know if she meant crying or what. "Why'd you come down?"

I was watching her eyes, the way they filled up from the bottoms.

Come on, Goodman. You know what she wants you to say.

That I came down to see her.

So say it.

It's pretty easy for me to lie. People usually believe me. So I try to tell the truth. Not that I'm Tom Hanks or anything. I just think you should tell the truth. If you can. Of course, maybe people only pretend to believe me.

I said, "I came down for two reasons." What a fence-sitter. "To see how you were and to get my car keys." That was handy, remembering she had my car keys.

But she said, "I gave them back to you at the house. Remember? They're in your coat pocket."

Now what? I couldn't just say, Hey, Em, your job's in trouble.

I got out a cigarette. She asked for one and I gave her the pack. They were hers anyway. She tried to give them back to me. I said, "No, you keep them, they're yours."

"It's okay."

"I got them in your kitchen."

She said, "I know. It's okay."

"Will you quit saying it's okay?" Did she think I couldn't buy my own cigarettes?

"I'm sorry."

"And don't be sorry." I practically yelled it. I looked up at Mike's window and I swear I saw the curtain move.

She said, "You better go back up."

"Okay." As soon as it came out, we both started to laugh.

"Em, don't go thinking it's your fault."

"What?"

That Mike's thinking of firing you, I thought. But that's not what I said. What I said was, "Any of it."

"You mean last night?"

Before I even thought about it, I said, "I had a great time last night."

"Me, too." She smiled. "Did Mike say anything? I bet Katrina couldn't wait to tell him you were there this morning."

Was that how he knew? I said, "Well, I sort of told him myself. But he already knew. He knew a long time ago."

"That was when everybody knew and it wasn't true!" Funny, but I understood what she meant. She said, "Is that why he made me leave?"

Did she think it was fun staying? I said, "He didn't *make* you leave, he's *letting* you leave."

"Bullshit." She glared at me.

She's right, Goodman. Mike did want her out of there.

Is that my fault?

Probably not. And you probably don't want her to think it is.

I don't know what I want. Not from Em or from Mike. I said, "He's going to ask you to do something."

"What?"

"I don't know."

"You don't know shit, do you, Goodman?"

"I know I felt great this morning." It just came out. I guess I was tired of her yelling at me. I dropped my cigarette and stepped on it.

She said, "You don't have any socks on." She was sitting on the top of her car seat like a homecoming queen.

I thought, What the hell. So I said, "'You mind if I come by later? Maybe look for my socks?"

She grinned like a two-year-old. "That's exactly what I was thinking." Then she leaned down and kissed me.

I kissed her back. She probably thought I was saying okay.

CHAPTER 35 ◆ SEETHING WITH INTERNAL EMOTIONS, SHE WAITS ◆

I went shopping. I bought oysters, smoked sausages, salmon mousse, goose pâté, blackberries, oranges, strawberries, brie, baguettes and chocolate eclairs. I bought everything I thought Bud might like. I also bought a bottle of Taittinger's. I was arranging it all on my counter so I could admire it when the phone rang.

It was Reek. "Have you spoken to Michael yet?" he asked.

"Yeah. We met with him this morning, as a matter of fact."

"And?"

"And what?" What did he want to know?

"Did he like the script, Emmaline?" He sounded impatient.

"Yeah, he did, as a matter of fact. He was very complimentary."

Reek made a noise, almost a grunt. "What about the rewrite?"

I tried to sound casual. "Mike and Bud are doing it."

"Mike and Bud? What about you?"

"Nothing about me. I came home."

"Why didn't *you* stay?"

"Because they didn't want me to." I hadn't meant to say that.

"What's the matter, Emmaline? Did they exclude you?"

"No, they didn't exclude me . . ."

"No girls allowed in the tree house?"

"Reek, I have to go now." I was getting a headache.

"What about the reading? Is it still on for Monday?"

"Mike didn't say. He didn't mention a reading at all."

"Hmmmmm."

I couldn't help myself. "What does that mean?" I asked.

"It means Monty may be getting to people."

I felt confused by this whole conversation. "Why?"

"To tell them to be, shall we say, less than cooperative? Monty has more power than certain people give him credit for."

This was getting ridiculous. "Reek, I really do wanna go lie down . . ."

"Excuse me. I thought you cared about what happened to your script. Which, by the way, I thought was very good."

"Then you did read it." He'd hinted as much last week, but when I'd tried to pin him down, he was elusive. Even now, he changed the subject.

"I'll call you later when I hear how the rewrite went," he said.

"That's okay, I'll find out." I should've kept my big mouth shut.

"Oh?" Of course, he picked up on it immediately; he wasn't a mini-mogul for nothing. "How?"

It was inevitable, I thought. "Bud's coming by later."

"Ooohhhhh." He could do a lot with one word.

"Get your mind out of the gutter, Reek."

"You stay out of my mind," he said. It had a odd ring to it. "But don't tire Bud out too much, you two have to be funny. God knows somebody has to."

This emotional roller coaster—the excitement, the disappointment, the irritation—was exhausting. It was like high school, when the class gossip finds out you have a secret date with the quarterback. You know everyone's going to find out; in a way, you hope they do. Reek definitely qualified as the class gossip. The guy knew *everything*.

I ran a bath and peeled off my clothes, thinking how perfect it would be if Bud walked in while I was in the tub. How sexy. How Marilyn Monroe. Or was it Sharon Stone? Who cared, it was bound to lead to fucking. I lit a joint.

I stretched out in the tub, banning any thoughts of Reek or the show from my mind. Bud would be here soon; we'd have a wonderful night. We had all day tomorrow, too. I closed my eyes and gave in to conjuring exquisite fantasies.

When I got out of the tub, I went into the bedroom and got out a black satin teddy I'd bought two years ago and never worn. It had spaghetti straps, ivory lace around the edges and snaps in the crotch.

I put on a long, black, silky robe, letting it hang open. I needed shoes, preferably a pair of those Barbie-doll mules with pompoms. The closest I had were flip-flops; I decided to go barefoot. I fixed my makeup, then glided into the living room. I lit some candles. It was eight o'clock.

I grabbed a cigarette and went out on the sunporch. The smog had made for another gorgeous sunset: orange and pink and blue and lavender. If he shows up right now, I thought, I won't say a word about doubting him. He *is* going to come. He *is*.

When I turned around to get an ashtray, I saw *Revenge of the Sand Castle*. I'd given Bud such a hard time about it. I picked up the bucket. It was heavy; sand weighs a ton. I lugged it over to the door, where he'd see it as soon as he walked in. I collected cigarette butts from ashtrays all over the house and I lovingly arranged them around the outstretched plaster-of-paris hand. I smiled, thinking I would tell Bud it was *handiwork*. When I finished, it was almost nine-thirty. I ate an eclair. Then I curled up on the rattan love seat and fell asleep.

CHAPTER 36 ◆ ME AND MY MOGUL ◆

Right off the bat, Mike said, "We need a new name." It came out, "We knee a nude naaymah."

"A new name," I said. "Instead of Happy?" He nodded, which meant his head bobbled up and back a little and then dropped down to his chest. Em loved the name *Happy*. I said, "Any ideas?"

His shoulders jerked up. A shrug, I think. It set off a chain reaction of twitches and shakes. "Something funny," he said.

"Okay." That meant something *he* thought was funny. "How about *Shlomo*?"

He grinned. "Too Jewish."

"*Olaf*. One of the great underused names in comedy, *Olaf*."

"Morty." It came out Mworr-dee.

"Morty?"

"Yeah. Like in, What do you want to do tonight, Morty?" He yukked it up.

I said, "Morty it is." I made a note on the script. "Hey, is someone coming in to take notes for us?"

"Later. Can you . . ." He waved his hand at my script.

"Sure." I finished making the note about the name change. "Now what?"

"I love my chair. Going up." He just got this new chair. He flipped a lever that works a hydraulic pump on the seat. It made a hissing noise and he went up about six inches. It's going to be a long day, I thought.

We moved slowly through the script. Mike'd pick out a line he didn't like, usually a joke that needed punching up. We didn't exactly bust our butts. He'd take the second or third or even first joke we'd try. I've seen him go through twenty or thirty before he liked one.

We took a lot of breaks, too. One when Katrina Rhinestone showed up. Another when he had to make a phone call. I almost called Em at the same time, but I figured I better wait till I knew what was going on. About four o'clock, he said, "You hungry?" We'd just finished a run where Morty talked about toothbrushes for a page and a half. Not necessarily better than what was there before, but different. That's what rewriting's about—sometimes you go sideways.

I said, "Not too hungry, no. Why don't we work through?"

"I missed my Wheaties this morning. You remember Heather." He grinned some more. I almost asked him if she really was a hooker. Mike loves to say that kind of stuff whether it's true or not.

I asked him, "You got a date later?" I was hoping he did. Then he'd want to knock off early.

But he said, "Naw. She was a pig anyway. Come on."

We went to the Imperial Gardens. Japanese food. Mike loves Japanese food. Personally, it all looks like bait to me.

As soon as we sat down, he ordered sake. Even though I said I didn't want any. When the waitress brought over two of those little bottles, Mike asked her for a straw. He usually carries his own, but I guess he forgot it. She watched him slurp up his sake like it was the most amazing thing she'd ever seen. Then we watched her walk back to the bar. She was wearing one of those kimonos and lots of makeup. Not white like a geisha girl or anything, just lots of regular makeup. A little red mouth.

Mike said, "You like Japanese pussy?"

I said, "Sure, you mean like Ferix the Cat?"

Mike started laughing and coughing at the same time. The waitress came over to pound his back. When he was finished choking, he said we were ready to order. He rattled something off and she asked him a question and then he rattled something else off. I wondered if he was any easier to understand in Japanese.

When the waitress left, he said, "Remember when we used to do this all the time? Get tanked with Gene Muncy?"

I said, "Sure." Gene used to get a kick out of Mike. He couldn't believe the way Mike'd toss them back. Once Gene gave him a platinum straw for a present. "Those were your pre-mogul days."

He said, "I like being a mogul."

That was no surprise. "It suits you. That's what the pinstripe said to the dummy, *It suits you.*" I was starting to feel the sake.

"How come we never do it any more? You and me? Going out like this?" He waved his arm at me. "You married that belly dancer!"

"I pled insanity, the judge let me off."

All of a sudden, Mike got up, started rolling his hips and humming "Little Egypt." People were staring, but Mike loves to attract attention. Not that he has any choice.

The waitress came back with Mike's sushi. She brought more sake, too. I said, "No more for me. I'm driving."

Mike said, "I'll drive." Cracked himself up.

You had to feel for Mike sometimes. When you realized he couldn't even do something like drive.

Then he said, "Tell me about Emmaline."

"What about her?"

"She a good writer?"

I couldn't tell if he was serious, really wanting to know or just setting me up. "Yeah," I said. "She is. Smart, funny. She's good at keeping you on story." Which is something I'm terrible at, but I didn't say that. Mike knows anyway.

"What about fucking?"

I hadn't realized how drunk he was. His eyes stayed closed when he blinked.

"You think you'll get laid tonight?"

His voice seemed really loud. I know everybody does it, talks about sex in public, but it seems, I don't know. I guess I'm old-fashioned. It just seems like bad manners to me.

"It's okay, Bud. In fact, it's good. Man should be laid! Man must be laid!" He pounded his fist on the table, standing up to do it right. People were rubbernecking all over the restaurant.

"Mike . . ." I tried to get him to quiet down.

He half-sat, half-fell. "Is my fly open?" he said. "With all this erotic talk I thought my fly might've burst open." He flung his arms out. "Hercules unchained!" Then he leaned forward, elbows sprawling, and knocked over the sake. The straw went on the floor, the sake went on him.

I let the waitress clean up. I went to the phone booth and called Reek.

He said, "Why should I come get him?"

I was glad he was home. "I'll owe you one, Reek."

"Don't think I won't collect." I told him where we were. He said, "I'm leaving now. "

I went back out to the table. Mike was standing there pulling money out of his pockets. Giving it to the waitress, who was giggling her head off. He said, "She's taking me home." He threw his arm around her and almost smacked her in the face. She giggled even more.

I said, "You teaching her English?"

"I'm teaching her French!" She started to lead him away. "We'll finish the rewrite tomorrow."

"Fine. 11:00?"

He looked at her, then at me. "Better make it 12:00. She looks like a slow learner." One thing about Mike, he never has any trouble getting girls.

When I got to Em's the lights were out. The door was unlocked so I went in. The next thing I know, I'm on the floor and there's sand in my mouth.

The lights went on and Em helped me up. She was practically naked. She picked up the bucket I'd tripped over. It was that sculpture.

"I'm sorry." I started helping her scrape up the sand. She showed me how she'd collected butts from all over the house and arranged them in the bucket. On account of how I used it as an ashtray before. A callback. "Funny," I said.

Then she said, "I'm glad you showed up."

"Did you think I wouldn't?" I had been thinking. Considering. Escape routes.

She said, "I knew you would."

For just a second, the way she said it, *I knew you would*, I thought about mindreading again. Her being able to. Then she moved toward me and started kissing me. Right in the spilled-out sand. And I stopped thinking about anything.

CHAPTER 37 ◆ GRAPPLING WITH LIFE'S LITTLE LESSONS ◆

I woke up when the sun hit me. I was lying on my side, one leg tangled up in Bud's. My head was resting in the crook of his shoulder, in that indentation between his neck and chest. He has a wonderful crook.

I moved my fingers over his chest. My favorite kind of chest is smooth, tan and hairless, like seventeen-year-old boys have. Those are fantasy chests though; Bud's chest had some darkish hair around each nipple, some in the middle, not enough to be hairy and not seventeen-looking either. It was a real-life chest.

I slid my hand down to his stomach. Hair ran down the center line, a fine row of Vs pointing to his navel. I followed it with my finger, stopping at his belly button. He had a nice, oval innie, the hair circling it gray and curly.

"Good morning," he said. One eye was open. Blue, but not icy-blue like Paul Newman's, more of a soft blue, almost gray-blue.

"Good morning."

"It's terrible out here," he said.

"Uh huh." We'd pulled some cushions down off the porch furniture, but the floor was hard and there was still sand everywhere. "You wanna move to another part of the beach?"

He grunted and grabbed his pants, pulling them on before he stood up.

"You'll get sand in your underwear," I said, but he ignored me. There were bamboo shades on the porch. I left my clothes off.

As we walked down the hall past the bathroom, I said, "Hey, in here."

"What for?" he asked.

"You look like a veal cutlet. "

He reached up to wipe sand off his shoulder. I helped him, then he helped me with the sand on my back. What with all the helping, and since I wasn't wearing anything, we kind of forgot about the shower. That's something Ned and I never did, make love in the bathroom.

I said, "I'll bet you save a lot of money on sheets." I pushed back the shower curtain to turn on the water. "You want to take a shower?"

"Together?" He made it sound unthinkable.

I laughed. "Don't worry, we'll be wearing blindfolds. I have these little black washcloths . . ." I stopped because he wasn't looking at me any more; then I noticed that even his back was blushing. "Shit, you're embarrassed."

"Well, I . . . you know . . . I mean . . ." He was stammering.

"Okay, never mind. You take a shower. When you get out, I'll have a wonderful breakfast all ready for you."

Bud said, "I can't stay for breakfast. I told Mike I'd meet him at noon."

"But it's Sunday."

He shrugged. "We have to finish the rewrite." I think his calm lack of concern got to me as much as anything.

"What the fuck did you do yesterday?"

"You know. We worked, but we didn't finish . . ."

I couldn't stand it. "Never mind." I stomped out of the bathroom, went into my room and grabbed my robe off the coatrack in the corner. Not my long, black, silky gown either, I wanted my dirty, ratty, old bathrobe with the hole in the elbow and the collar that didn't lay flat. The sleeve caught on a hook and the coatrack went crashing to the floor. I was aware of Bud watching me. I hated the way I was acting, but I couldn't seem to stop.

I slammed some pots around in the kitchen; that helped. After a few minutes, Bud came in. He didn't say anything, he just stood in the doorway, his hands in his pockets.

"Coffee?" My voice was neutral.

"That'd be nice." He watched me. It wasn't like Bud to look at me so directly for so long, and it was hard to meet his gaze. *All right,* I wanted to say, *I know I'm acting like an asshole. I feel hurt and left out and insecure.*

"Em." He came over to the counter. I let him put his arms around me, then was afraid I was going to cry.

"Shit," I said. It was a general comment.

"It's not my fault we didn't finish, honest. You know Mike. We did more talking than writing. I should've told you last night. I guess I got distracted." He smiled, shyly I thought.

"I remember." His hand slid inside my robe and down to my hip. I loved the way his hands felt on my skin. "Coffee's ready."

"Okay. Lots of cream and sugar, please."

I nodded. We sat across from each other at the kitchen table and both lit cigarettes. "So, how far did you guys get?" My voice actually sounded casual.

"Most of the first act," he said.

"Change much?"

"We added a run about toothbrushes. Couple of pages."

"Not instead of the phone-booth scene?" I'd kill them if they cut that; I loved that scene.

"No, after it. And what else? Oh, the big change . . ."

The phone rang, interrupting him. "Maybe it's Mike," I said. "He's calling to say forget the rewrite."

"Hello, Emmaline." It *was* Mike: no mistaking that voice.

"Hello, *Mike*." I smiled smugly at Bud. "How's it going?" He said something garbled. "Pardon me?"

"Better . . . than . . . can . . . be . . . expected," he said. He was even harder to understand over the telephone. "Is Bud there?"

Bud looked alarmed, but he took the receiver. I didn't want him to think I was eavesdropping, so I took my coffee and went into my office, where I keep my dope. I was almost done rolling a joint when Bud yelled from the kitchen, "He wants to talk to you now."

When I got to the phone, Mike asked if I were busy today.

"Not really. Why?"

"Why don't you join us for the rewrite? I think we can use your help."

What the fuck was he up to? "Okay."

Mike said, "Good. See you up fear."

There were several loud clicks as he tried to hang up.

Bud was standing there. I almost asked him whose idea this was, but I wasn't sure I wanted to know. Instead I asked, "Did you take a shower?"

"Why, is one missing?"

I shook my head. "Ba dump bump."

Then he asked, "You want to take one together?"

CHAPTER 38 ◆ MAGICIANS DO IT WITH MIRRORS ◆

We were almost to Mike's house when Monty Newman's car shot past us, going the other way. Doing about sixty in a thirty-mile zone.

"Why the hell was he up here?" We were in Bel Air, Monty lives in Encino.

What do you think, Goodman? The Star was visiting the Mogul.

Em said, "Maybe it was just someone who looks like Monty."

Right. In a yellow Corvette just like Monty's. But I let it go. If she didn't want to believe it was Monty Newman, it wasn't my job to make her.

We pulled into Mike's driveway. He was waiting for us, dribbling a basketball. Em laughed when she saw him. She was probably thinking that Mike playing basketball was a joke. She was wrong. I don't know if it's on account of the C. P., but Mike is the most competitive guy I know. He always plays to win.

As we got out of the car, Mike let the ball fly. He doesn't jump exactly, and I happen to know it's not a regulation-height basket, but it swished.

Em yelled, "Two points for the home team!"

I caught the ball, sent it back to Mike nice and easy. He dribbled it behind his back. Trying to impress Em. "Physical therapy class," he said. Making a joke. Like it wasn't nearly impossible, what he was doing.

After a while, he gave her the tour. Pointing out the pool, telling her how the house used to belong to a cowboy star named Rockabye Something or other. I headed for the greenhouse. That's where he always sets up the food.

I was on my second plateful when they showed up. Em helped him get his food. At work his secretary usually gives him a hand, sometimes Reek. Mike was telling Em to load up lots of herring. "I love herring," he said.

Our script was sitting on the table. Em spotted it right away. Mike said, "Why don't you read through it now? It'll give you an idea of where we are."

She was nodding. "Does it have the changes you made yesterday?"

Mike said, "Yeah."

I could see the clean pages. He sure had it redone fast. I guess I could've asked him what his hurry was. Or I could've asked him about Monty. Instead I listened to him talk about the new rookie the Lakers picked up out of Alabama State.

When Em finished reading, she said, "You guys added some funny shit."

Mike nodded. "Bud's the best."

She said, "Yeah, he is."

I felt like I was in the middle of something, but I didn't know what. Mike was still watching her. Waiting.

She said, "The second act seems rough."

We didn't do anything to the second act, I almost said. I didn't get a chance to. Mike was nodding.

Agreeing with her. "The second act does have problems."

Then she asked, "What about the name? Morty?" Real casual, she said, "Don't you think it's too close to Monty? It might look like a deliberate slap in the face."

He said, "I hope it does." Laughed. We laughed too. Only I was wondering how that fit in with Monty's visit.

Then Mike said, "I'm worried about the network. Their reaction has been favorable so far, but they're nervous about the new concept." Mike loves words like that, concept.

Em said, "You always seem able to reassure people. Make them feel comfortable. "

Mike told her, "I don't know if I want them to feel comfortable."

She looked over at me. This was the real Mike talking, I wanted to say. Of course, I didn't. I didn't say anything. Truth of the matter is, my mind started to wander.

It was a lucky day when Fate steered Emmaline Goldman Grosvenor into the Lanetti stable. The premiere episode of the refurbished *Life With Lucky* was co-written by the youthful, intelligent Ms. Grosvenor, who brings to her work a sharpness of wit and concept. Her partner in this endeavor, Bud Goodman, is an old hack, and he must surely appreciate the boost Grosvenor has given his flagging career.

In addition to her success in the workplace, the well-dressed Ms. Grosvenor seems to have hit it big on the social scene. She and Mike Lanetti are often seen together at the city's hot spots. "We share an interest in Italian sports cars," she quipped recently.

Suddenly I heard her ask Mike, "So where do we start rewriting?"

And he said, "I don't think we need to." He caught her off-guard, too. He said, "I wanted to get your reactions to the script. Which I did. Now we'll send it to the network. Spread the word to the cast. The sooner they know we're going ahead without Monty, the better."

"What about a reading?" she asked. "Someone told me there might be a reading tomorrow."

While I was wondering who she meant, Mike said, "That reminds me, what did you think of *Bigelow's Boys?*"

Em made a face like she got a bad piece of herring. "Pretty shitty. If you don't mind my saying so."

Mike shrugged, his shoulders pulling his body backward. "Can you be specific?"

She could. She was. I listened to her for a while. I hadn't even read the script, and I probably wouldn't. I watched Mike to see how he was taking it. As usual, it was hard to tell. When she was done, he nodded, and asked her if she'd write it all up for him, her opinions. "Sure," she said.

Pretty soon after that, he walked us out to the car. She thanked him for brunch and the tour of his house. He said, "I hope you don't think your time was wasted because we didn't write."

"Oh no," she said.

Then he said, "You better take it easier on Bud. After all, he's an old man." He was grinning, his lips pulled wide and his eyes bulging. And Em, I couldn't believe it, she was blushing. Guttermouth Grosvenor was blushing!

We got in the car. I backed down the driveway, wondering what she thought of him. I didn't have to wait long. She said, "What an incredible fucking guy."

"Yeah. That's what he is all right."

"He didn't really answer my question about the reading, did he?"

Of course he didn't. "Who did you mean when you said someone told you there might be a reading?"

"Reek," she said, sounding casual. "I thought you said you guys never got to the second act."

"We didn't."

"Someone did."

"What do you mean?"

"Someone rewrote parts of the second act." She took out her cigarettes. "Want one?"

I shook my head. Who the hell rewrote the second act?

"It's sure better not to trust any of them, isn't it?" she said.

Trust them? I wasn't sure I remembered *how* to trust them.

CHAPTER 39 ◆ I SHOULD HAVE KNOWN: IF YOU DON'T GET THE BLUES ON MONDAY, YOU GET THEM SOMEPLACE ELSE ◆

I know most people hate Mondays, but I love them. I feel like the week is stretching out in front of me, brand-new and unused. The world's still full of possibilities on a Monday.

I got out my new silk suit; nothing makes me feel better than wearing something new. The suit looked gorgeous, but it's this odd salmon color. I had to try on four blouses before I remembered the one I'd bought my friend Claire for her birthday but hadn't mailed yet. It was perfect, a pale pink, and although it was sheer, I knew I'd be wearing my jacket all day. They run the air conditioner in the office constantly and I usually freeze my ass off. My hair was easy; it was still too short to do anything but curl around my head like bits of left-over mohair. I tortured it with some mousse and then gave up.

I got to work about nine forty-five, and I was crossing the parking lot when a voice said, "Hello, pretty lady!"

It was Adalbert Argus, the actor who plays Pops. "Good morning." I waited for him to catch up with me and kissed him on the cheek.

"Watch out," he said. "My blood pressure."

We headed toward the office. "I thought the cast was still on hiatus," I said.

"I'm doing a voice-over. Some animated show."

"How cool. Is it fun?"

He shrugged. "I don't have to shave. How's the new script going? You write me something good?"

I thought about it; he didn't have much. "If it's still in," I lied. "You know how those fucking rewrites are."

"Sounds exciting."

"Don't be so literal. Remember your blood pressure."

We said good-bye and I went upstairs. Bud wasn't in our office. There was, however, a note on my desk from Peggy saying there was a staff meeting in the conference room. I took my cigarettes and my styrofoam cup of coffee and walked down the hall.

The other writers were already there. Bud looked terrible. He had big circles under his eyes and his skin was gray. There was an empty seat across the table from him, which I took.

"How are you?" I asked.

"I'm lousy," he said. "That's how I know I'm awake."

I looked around the table. Nyles Petersen nodded at me and said hi; I said hi back. "What're we waiting for?" I asked him.

"Mike. He's meeting with the network."

"Oh."

There was a plate of Danish in the center of the table. Rudankowitz, who was just finishing one, leaned forward and took another.

Bud said, "If Tuesday Weld married Fredric March and they had a daughter and named her after her mother, she'd be Tuesday, March the second."

He really was in bad shape. I wanted to say something to calm him down, touch his hand or something, but I knew that was a bad idea in front of everyone.

I should never have left him alone after the meeting at Mike's. I had to, though; I was dangerously close to saying I loved him. I almost said it when he dropped me off, it was right on the tip of my tongue. *I love you,* I almost said. *Come upstairs and I'll show you.*

I'll make it up to him, I thought. I'll get him alone in our office. I pictured myself shutting the door and moving closer to him. I'd kiss him, he'd kiss me back. Then I'd fuck his brains out, right there on our couch. That ought to cheer him up. It cheered me up just thinking about it. In fact, fantasizing about Bud actually allowed me to sit there and watch Rudankowitz eat the entire plate of Danish. I could transcend, for chrissake.

CHAPTER 40 ◆ WATCH YOUR FLANKS ◆

Emmaline came in late. She took the seat right across from me. We sat there a while. All of us watching Rudankowitz stuff his face with Danish. Then Emmaline said, "Christ, it's hot in here. What happened to the air conditioner?" She was right, it was hot.

"This room's on a separate blower," Pfeiffer told her. He thinks he's mechanical.

She said, "It's so stuffy." Then she took her jacket off. For crying out loud, she wasn't even wearing a bra.

Neiderhoff said, "It's stuffy because you all smoke too much."

I said, "Why don't you turn the blower on, Joe? It'll get rid of some of the smoke." Plus which, maybe Em would put her jacket back on.

All of a sudden, Murray, the scarf director, comes running in. He's out of breath, and he says, "Mike's on his way up." Like a kid telling the class the teacher's coming. Em lit a cigarette. I swear she blew the smoke right in Neiderhoff's face.

Sure enough, a minute later, Mike gimped in. Reek right behind him. They both looked serious. Full of important news.

It wasn't Mike's style to come right out with it. He walked to the head of the table and sat down. That took ten minutes. He blew his nose. Looked around the table. Then he said, "The network . . . wants to . . . abandon . . . the show." That was it.

For a second, it was completely quiet. Then they all started talking at once.

"Jesus, can they do that?"

"I thought they were behind us a hundred percent."

"Does this mean they buy us off?"

"Christ, we got a forty share last week."

"Against reruns."

"Is this final or what?"

"Do the actors know?"

"I thought they were behind us a hundred percent."

Mike just sat there. Letting them get it all out, I guess. After a while, he held up his hand. They stopped.

Except Emmaline. Of course. She said, "What's the story, Michael?" When did she start calling him Michael?

He waved his arm at Reek, who was leaning against the wall. Reek said, "They're afraid the show is irretrievably weakened by Monty Newman's defection. Monty appeals to demographics across the board. He has an unbelievably high TVQ."

"What's a TVQ?" Em asked.

"Television Quotient," Reek told us. "Primarily based on recognition factors." It occurred to me that Reek might actually know what he was talking about. "People who have never watched *Life With Lucky* still know who Monty Newman is."

"You mean his mother," I said.

No one laughed. Reek said, "For whatever reason, Monty resonates with the public."

Resonates. What the hell does that mean? "You think it's catching?"

"Unfortunately, no." Reek actually made a joke. Almost a joke. "They're also worried about Monty jumping ship. There are rumors he's pitching a show to Fox."

That set off another flurry. I looked at Mike. Sonuvagun, is that what Monty was doing at Mike's? Were the two of them in cahoots on another goddam show?

Everyone was yelling and talking at once. Em was right in the thick of it. Not me. I didn't have the guts.

Gutless Goodman is exactly what its title implies: gutless. Subtitled *An Autobiography of a Hack*, the book was written, author Bud Goodman claims, "because I hoped someone else could learn from my lousy example." Nice try, Mr. Goodman, but we've seen it done before. Better.

On to more exciting news in the literary world: Mike Lanetti and Emmaline Grosvenor have announced the opening of yet another branch of their internationally famous Good Writers' School. This campus, their fifteenth, is in Gstaad. "We prefer the term *clinic,*" Lanetti told this reporter over a double martini. "After all, the writers who come to us for help are, for the most part, sick. At least, their prose is."

Grosvenor agrees. "Of course, some people can never be cured of bad writing. For example, Bud Goodman, our ex-colleague, flunked out of seven different courses of treatment. Some people, obviously, cannot be helped."

"So, Michael, what's the bottom line?" Em.

Mike lurched back in his chair. "They expressed their concerns. I defended my staff."

Murray, the director, said, "What are the chances of Monty coming back?"

Mike exploded. "None! Monty Newman is not coming back!"

Murray froze. He didn't even blink.

Em said, "Look, I know I'm new to the show, but it's been in the top ten for three years, and notwithstanding Monty's TVQ, I don't think we need him. We have an opportunity to create something brand new here, something exciting that we think is good and funny."

Rudankowitz said, "There's a time to be practical too, Emmaline. Cut our losses."

"Maybe," Em said. "But remember what Michael said the day Monty quit?" She looked right at the Mogul. "You said we didn't need a star. You said *you* could make anyone a star."

That clinched it.

"Okay," Mike said. "But we've got a lot of work ahead of us. And despite what you think, Emmaline, we do need someone to play Morty." He swiveled around to Reek. "Get help if you need it. Call Harding and Horn in New York. You have until Friday. Got it?"

"Got it," Reek said. No emotion on his face at all, a sure sign he was pissed.

Then for the rest of us, Mike said, "We start rewriting this afternoon. Table at 2:00." He pounded the script with his fist. People nodded and tried to get out of the room.

It was a quarter after twelve and I was thinking maybe Chinese food. Em caught up with me out in the hallway. "Got a minute, Bud?"

I said, "Sure. How about Chinese?"

"Sounds good. Can I talk to you first? In our office?" She had a funny look on her face.

We went in the office and she closed the door. Leaned against it.

I said, "I guess we all owe you our jobs, huh? You convinced him."

She said, "I couldn't convince Mike that shit stinks if he didn't already believe it." She paused, then added, "But maybe I do deserve a reward."

I said, "Yeah, well . . ."

I didn't get to finish. Not that I could've talked anyway. My mouth was all of a sudden full of her. She knocked me over. Right onto the couch. And launched herself on top of me.

Can you believe it, Goodman? After all these years. And all those fantasies about having a couch in the office. You finally get to use it.

CHAPTER 41 ◆ I'LL THINK OF A TITLE LATER; UNTIL THEN, FUCK OFF ◆

There's a moment right after sex when you can actually *feel* the connection to another person. It's not just physical, either; it's about communication. The lines are open and direct. I've always thought if mind reading were possible, that's when it would happen, right after making love.

I stretched. I wanted to stay on that couch, my belly rubbing against Bud's, for the rest of our lives. So when I asked how he felt, and he said, "Like I never felt on Christmas," I wondered, What does that mean? And I said, "What does that mean?" Direct lines: think it, say it.

"Well..." He seemed embarrassed. "Remember Christmas morning? You'd come downstairs and see all those presents. Boxes. Ribbons. The Christmas tree lit up. And it was all just waiting for you. Anything was possible."

"Uh huh." We didn't celebrate Christmas in my family, but I wanted him to go on.

"Then it starts. First, they make you put on your bathrobe before you can open anything. Then the boxes have underwear in them. Or socks. Don't tear the paper. Wait your turn. Don't make such a mess."

I'd been running my finger over Bud's wet belly and I said, "It's fun to make a mess," at the same exact instant he said, "It's fun to make a mess." Talk about direct communication. Bud, I love you.

Shit, can't say that. Close your mouth and put your head down. Relax. Think about communication, how it's possible, how *anything's* possible.

Then Bud said, "Em, do you really care?"

About you? I assumed that's what he meant, and I almost said it, "About you?" There must've something in my look, though, because he added, "You know, about the show. "

The *show*? "Sure I care." I said.

He shrugged. "I just wondered. What you said at the meeting, about creating something new and exciting. Did you mean that?"

Shit. I'm lying here thinking about making a connection with you, achieving an actual *relationship*, and you're talking about thirty-two pages that need punching up. I said, "I don't say shit I don't mean." I started to get dressed.

"What's wrong?"

166

"Nothing. Look, it's a quarter to two. If we're going to be on time for this asshole meeting, we'd better get moving."

"Yeah, okay." He picked his pants up off the floor and pulled them on. Then he looked thoughtful. I watched him, and for the second time, I thought he was going to talk about us, about what we could do, what we were doing. Instead he said, "See, the way I figure it, if the network cancels the show, Mike doesn't have to pay us off. But if it's his decision to stop the show, we're all still under contract."

"Bud, I don't want to hear any more mogul-move shit. You're like one of those Kennedy conspiracy nuts."

"I'm just saying Mike's waiting for the network to cancel us and the network is waiting for Mike to fire us. A Mexican standoff. Don't tell Reek I said that though."

"And *I* think if Mike's going to shake things up, I'd rather stay on *Life With Lucky* where it's our script and we have a chance to wield a little power." I'd called Ken Harris last night and found out my deal *was* with Lanetti Enterprises; Mike could move me anywhere he wanted. "I certainly don't want to go over to *Bigelow's Boys*, for chrissake. Did you know Rudankowitz and Pfeiffer wrote that piece of shit? And Rosa says they're in line to produce it if *Lucky* gets canceled."

Bud was motionless, staring at me.

"What's the matter?"

"When did you figure all this stuff out?"

He was so easily impressed. "You don't need to be a mogul to have moves." I put my shoes on and stepped into my skirt. One of my heels caught in the hem and ripped out a good two inches. "Shit!"

"Here, let me . . ."

167

"Don't!"

"I could go down to wardrobe . . ."

"Just leave me alone!"

We both stood there, frozen. Damn it, it *is* possible to communicate. Why didn't he understand that?

I reached underneath my skirt to pull down my blouse. Just then our office door flew open. It was Reek.

"Michael's about to start . . ." He trailed off, giving us an arched-eyebrow leer. "And what have you two been doing?"

"Reek," I said, "go fuck yourself."

"That's what I thought you were doing." He left, shutting the door. Christ, I thought, we didn't even lock it.

Then Bud said, "You think we should go in separately? To the meeting?"

I forced myself to sound casual. "Sure." I summoned the remnants of my dignity; that took a nanosecond. I paused in the doorway, remembering that line he used to say all the time. "Life is a series of small humiliations ending in a large one. Right, Bud?"

He was stunned. "How did you . . . ? I was about to say that, I swear."

"Let's just say I know what you're thinking."

If he was stunned before, he was flabbergasted now. I swept past him, and all I could think was, thank God I didn't say I loved him.

CHAPTER 42 ◆ SHE KNOWS ◆

She said it. She knows what I'm thinking. Geez, what am I going to do now?

Nothing, Goodman. It's the one thing you're good at.

Why'd I have to jump her bones in the office?

You were off your form, that's all. The couch, the walls: you had to hold back. Tell you what you do. You forget all about Emmaline, you go down to the marina, find a nice-looking stewardess. Buy her half a dozen of those banana daiquiris, whatever that stuff is they drink. You get your confidence back.

Remember that first time with her? It was like we were inside each other's brains. It was like being transported.

You want to be transported, Goodman, take a bus. Go to the marina. You'll have fun, you'll get laid.

There's a big difference between getting laid and making love.

Have you been watching Oprah again?

We were all in the conference room. Waiting. She walks in with Mike on one side of her and Reek on the other. The three of them yukking it up. She wouldn't say anything to them about us. Would she?

Why not, Goodman? She probably sold Mike the movie rights.

"Is everyone ready to start?" That was Mike. The Mogul always gets the first line at a meeting.

"Before we do, I have something interesting to report." It was Murray, the scarf director. What was he doing here?

Mike said, "Yes?"

Murray said, "I had lunch with several members of the cast." Real quick he added, "It wasn't my idea. They were waiting for me out in the parking lot. They wanted to know what was going on." Murray was feeling good. He had everyone's attention.

Then Mike said, "I hope you didn't tell them anything, Murray."

Which made Murray real nervous. He tried to puff on his cigarette. Only it stuck to his bottom lip. He said, "Well, I didn't give them any details, Mike. I just spoke generally, told them the network was nervous, but you were committed."

"Terrific. Now I'm going to have a bunch of actors phoning me. And their agents phoning me. You want to take those calls, Murray?"

Murray shook his head. He looked awful. He said, "I'm sorry, Mike, I didn't realize. Arnie Dish said they deserved to know what was going on."

"Actors don't deserve to breathe," Mike said. "And directors are all just frustrated actors. Now, shall we see what we have to do to save this show?"

It was a great way to start the rewrite.

Em spoke up right away. "We were talking before about starting Act Two in the candy store. We could do the phone call—there's a phone booth in the candy store, right? Get something going between Pops and Morty. Adalbert has virtually nothing in the script."

I flipped through the pages. She was right about Adalbert. When did she notice that?

"Yeah. Pops could be giving him advice or something." That was from Nyles Petersen.

"Perfect," Em said. "On how to get along in the neighborhood." She looked from Nyles back to Mike.

Mike frowned. His eyebrows came down and nearly closed his eyes. "What kind of advice? Good advice?"

Em said, "Maybe it's funnier if it's bad advice."

Nyles agreed. "Bad advice is always funny."

Neiderhoff chimed in. "Pops wouldn't give him bad advice." Like he knows.

Em said, "Maybe Pops gives him what he thinks is good advice, but Morty blows it. That way we get the comedy and a lesson, too. Be yourself."

She looked around at everyone. They were waiting to see what Mike would say.

Mike nodded. He liked it. "Okay, so Pop gives him bad advice. Funny bad advice."

Then Reek came into the conference room. He walked over to Mike and whispered something in his ear. Mike nodded and then straightened up. "I have to take this phone call. Back in five minutes, everybody."

Mike and Reek left and then Em was waving at me, making this sign that she needed to talk to me. We went out in the hallway. She said, "I just wanted to apologize. I got mad before . . ."

"You don't have to . . ."

"I want to," she interrupted. She looked around. The hall was empty. She said, "Do you remember that night you showed me the train station? Then we went back to my place?"

That was the first time we did it. "I remember," I said.

"And do you remember what you said about our script? You said it proved it was possible for people to communicate."

Transported. "I said that?"

She smiled. "Yes. I think we really have a shot at that. I think it is possible. And . . . about fighting? Everybody fights. It's part of communicating. Even Ozzie and Harriet must've had fights, right?"

I said, "Sure. After Dave and Ricky went to bed." I remembered what it was like being on the couch with her. "Em, I think . . ." Christ, I almost said it. *I think I love you.* What's going on here? I said, "It's hard, Em . . ."

"No, it's not."

"It is. You don't know . . ."

"I'm looking right at it," she said. "It's not hard." She was pointing at my, you know, crotch.

Then Katrina stuck her head around the corner. "Mike's ready."

I looked at Em. "I'll get you later," I said.

She smiled. "I'm counting on it," she said.

Back inside the conference room, Mike was standing up at his end of the table. He glanced at us, then said, "Something's come up. I have to leave." He turned to glare at Murray, who was standing against the wall with his head down.

"What should we do?" That was Rudankowitz.

"Finish the rewrite," Mike said. "That'll be the schedule this week. The cast will rehearse . . . right, Murray?" Murray nodded quickly. Mike looked back at us. "And you'll rewrite. Got it?"

"Who's going to run the table?" Rudankowitz again. "Is Mel coming back?"

"Mel is *definitely* not coming back," Mike said, "Bud will do it."

That was a surprise. Which in a way made it no surprise. Moguls love to spring things on you.

CHAPTER 43 ◆ IT ALL COMES TOGETHER ◆

Neiderhoff was at the refrigerator, demanding to know who took his Orangina. Heywood said, "You know, some shows get all kinds of gourmet snacks."

Franks nodded. "Jim Brooks orders fresh fruit every day, delivered from Jurgensen's."

"Hey," I said, "we've got a bag of Cheetos!"

Nyles opened the bag and studied a Cheeto carefully. "You think it's true," he asked, "they make these out of Styrofoam?"

"I've got a better question," I said. "Why do you call the rewrite a table?" I was genuinely curious, but they looked at me like it was a set up for a missing punch line. "I mean it, how come?"

No one knew. Nyles said, "I guess the table's the most important ingredient. Otherwise we'd be holding our scripts on our laps." I liked Nyles.

Bud kind of coughed then. We all looked at him and he shrugged. "I guess we should get started. We're on this coffee thing, page eighteen." He turned to Katrina. "Did you have some notes?"

Katrina consulted her steno pad, her script, went back to the pad, and finally read aloud. "Get a new coffee thing."

"Try a percolator," Rudankowitz bellowed.

"That's funny," said Pfeiffer. He wasn't being sarcastic either. That's what comedy writers say. They rarely laugh; instead they say, "That's funny." That's why every writer worth a nickel obsesses over making other writers laugh. The best audience is the one that's hardest to get.

Bud began to murmur. "Pops pouring coffee. Coffee grounds. Grounds for divorce. Coffee beans. Earning beans. Counting beans. Jumping beans."

"Pops pours coffee," said Nyles. "Gets some on Morty. Says, It's okay, this stuff is a great spot remover."

"Or the other way," said Franks. "He spills some and says, Watch out, this stuff'll eat through steel."

"Pops wouldn't say that—he loves his coffee." That was Neiderhoff.

I said, "What if Pops says, You take cream?, and Morty says, Why, is it missing?"

Heywood said, "What if Morty says, How about some coffee?, and Pops says, No thanks, I've had plenty."

"How about Pops says, You take sugar?, and Morty says, Why, is it missing?" That was from Neiderhoff. No one even looked at him.

"Got it," said Nyles. "Pops says, There's nothing like a great cup of coffee. And Morty says, Yeah, you know where I can get one?"

"That's funny."

"Good." Bud nodded to Katrina, whose job it was to transcribe the changes.

"Uh oh." I suddenly realized we'd overlooked something. "We need a new title." The cover of the script still read *Happy Go Lucky*.

"I always liked this title," Neiderhoff said.

"It's a stupid title," Rudankowitz sneered.

"How about something with Morty in it?" Nyles suggested.

"Morty Strikes Out," Rudankowitz said.

"Morty Strikes Back," I said.

Bud shrugged; he liked it. He nodded to Katrina, who made the change. Then he said, "Okay, about this scene with Pops. We have to lose almost all of scene four, write new . . ."

"You can't!" Rudankowitz shouted.

"What's the matter?" asked Pfeiffer, instantly alert.

"We'll lose the run about the candy store!" Rudankowitz was turning the pages of the script, looking from Bud to me accusingly.

"That's a great run," said Neiderhoff. As if he'd recognize one.

"We'll save what we can," said Bud.

I was looking over the scene. It was fucking awkward anyway, because everyone was in it; when you have six people in a scene, it's hard to keep them all alive. Besides, we wanted Arnie, Pete and Chip to leave so we could do the scene with Pops and Morty. So I said, "What if Pops tells them, I started this candy store with next to nothing. Twenty years later, I've built it up to *less* than nothing."

"Good cut," Nyles said, looking at the script.

Bud nodded and started to say something to Katrina.

"That run is important to the history of the show!" yelled Rudankowitz. As if we had viewers compiling a timeline of when Pops started selling creamsicles.

"Get a life, Marvin," I said.

"Easy for you," he sneered. "I don't notice *your* stuff getting cut."

"That's enough," Bud said. The edge of reprimand in his voice was so uncharacteristic that we were all instantly silent. Bud hated confrontation. Now his expression was grim. "Maybe it's a good thing you brought this up, Marvin. Maybe it needs to be out in the open."

I didn't dare look around. Bud's fingers fiddled with the pages spread out in front of him. "Some of you," he said, "may be feeling like I'm showing some kind of . . . what's the word? Favoritism. You may even think it's based on something, you know, sexual. I want to say right now. So there won't be any doubt. There is nothing going on between Nyles and me."

As everybody laughed, his smile flickered up at me. I felt as if life couldn't get any better.

CHAPTER 44 ◆ IT ALL FALLS APART ◆

The thing of it is, I should've seen it coming. I mean, if you're feeling good, something's bound to fall apart. Sooner or later. Naturally, in my case, it would be sooner.

It was Friday. We'd made it through the week with the tables and all that. I was trying to figure a way to talk to Em about the weekend. I had these plans. Then she said she wanted to go see how the casting was going. And I went along to see, too. On account of being such a weak-kneed idiot.

We tape on Stage 4. Which is pretty much an empty warehouse. Plus which, it's always freezing. In a corner there's a set and some lights. If it's a show like ours where they use an audience for the taping, they lug in bleachers and a busload of folks from a nursing home. Welcome to showbiz.

Mike was sitting up in the bleachers. The stairs are tricky; I don't know why he'd want to go up there instead of sitting down in the front row. He had Katrina Rhinestone on one side and that receptionist, Sahndra, on the other side. Two girls to give notes to. Any self-respecting mogul has at least two girls. Maybe it took two just to understand him.

The truth of the matter is, he didn't have to be there at all. He could've watched tapes. But he was making some kind of mogul-production of it. There were a couple of network guys there, too. The question is, were they there because of Mike, or was Mike there because of them? Who was keeping an eye on who? Whom?

Em and I stood by the door. Some actor was just finishing. Squinting around. When he saw Mike, he started pleading. "Please, Mr. Lanetti, I know I can do better."

Mike said, "It was fine." With his voice so bored you could tell he didn't care if it was fine or not. He said something else, low. Both girls wrote it down.

But the actor wouldn't leave. He said, "Please, Mr. Lanetti. I was just nervous."

Mike ignored him. Reek picked up the cue. That's what he's paid to do, pick up cues. "We're on a super-tight schedule," he said to the actor. Only the actor wouldn't budge. He wanted his chance over again. That's why I hate to watch actors. Too much pain in one spot.

"You were great." It was Emmaline. Talking so loud everyone could hear.

The actor looked at her. "Really? I was okay?"

"Absolutely," Em said. "Thank you for coming." She waved at the actor. Who waved back and finally left. I thought Mike was going to say something to her, but he only looked down at Katrina's notes.

"I thought you wanted to be here," I whispered to Em.

"I do. I want to see how this friend of mine does."

"You won't see anything if they make us leave."

Just then Sahndra looked over at us. She actually put her finger up to her lips to say "Shhhh."

I could almost feel Em about to say something, but just then Reek came back. He said to Mike, "You ready for another one?"

Mike shook his head. "Naw. Let's break for lunch." He hauled himself up and headed down the stairs,

Katrina Rhinestone and Sahndra Fingerlips following close. It was like watching a toddler walk, the way they hovered right next to him, waiting to catch him if he fell.

Reek came over to us. He looked tired and pissed. "What are you two doing here?"

"We've got nothing better to do," I said.

Reek rolled his eyes. "What I meant was, these sessions are closed."

"We're the writers," Em said. Like that counted for anything. Then she headed for Mike.

The Mogul was surrounded by a clump of network suits. Discussing different actors. Looking at pages of names and notes. Em said, "Has Stu Young read yet?"

Mike gave me a look that Em didn't see. Plus which, she sounded so sure of herself, she had the suits all looking through their notes. Finally this one guy said, "Stuart Young, yes, he read at 9:00."

"Isn't he good?" she said.

"He was black," one of the suits said. Surprised.

Em nodded. "Right. We want ethnic, don't we?"

"Come on, Em," I said, "I'm starved."

She ignored me. She said to Mike, "Did you like him?" Putting him right on the spot. Mike was practically wild-eyed. Of course, I don't know if anyone but Reek and I could tell. Em obviously couldn't.

Then one of the suits said, "Morty's supposed to be Lucky's cousin. How can he be Lucky's cousin if he's black?"

Em smiled. "Big family?" Great, now she was being a wiseass. She said, "We could always rewrite the script."

That did it. I grabbed her by the elbow and dragged her out. When we got to the hallway she pulled away from me. "What the fuck are you doing?" she asked.

"Trying to save your ass."

"Thank you, I can save it myself."

I said, "Then why don't you?"

"What do you mean?"

"Nothing. You do what you want." I headed down the hall.

She followed me. "Bud, what's the matter?"

I didn't know what to say. I knew if I opened my mouth, something really nasty'd come out. So I just kept quiet.

We went through an outside door. Wound up on a concrete landing with a couple of steps. I don't know where we were. Facing the back of the lot, I think. At least we were outside. There was a gray metal railing and I leaned my elbows on it.

Em said, "You want a cigarette?"

"Em, don't mess up what we've got."

She looked at me for a minute, then she lit her cigarette. "You mean all this?" Waving her arm at the view.

"Fine. Forget it." I started down the steps.

She called after me. "Okay, okay, what am I doing wrong?"

"Quit harassing Mike. I'm serious, Em. You back him into a corner, all he'll do is come out fighting."

"What does that have to do with us?"

I said, "For pete's sake, you need an economics lesson?"

"We can always get other jobs, Bud."

I've only ever worked for two people in show-biz, Gene Muncy and Mike Lanetti. Who else was going to hire me? I said, "I like my job, Emmaline."

"I like mine, too. So?" Then she said, "Is that what you're talking about—our jobs? Because I thought you were talking about us. That's what you said. Don't mess up what we have."

I thought, What do we have, Em? But that's not what I said. I said, "I was talking about Mike. You don't stand a chance against him."

She said, "How do you know?" She blew smoke out slowly.

I said, "For one thing, you're not that good a liar."

She dropped her cigarette and stepped on it. Smiled. Then said, "Come on, I bet you're starving."

Mike was holding court in the middle of the commissary. Every so often he likes to mingle with the commoners. I should've known we were in trouble when Em led the way to join him.

They were talking about casting. The Scarf would bring up a name and Mike would say how much the network hated whoever it was.

Em said, "You know who I thought the best one reading was?"

My ears perked up. *She's stirring it up again.*

She said, "Reek."

"Who?" the Scarf asked.

"Enrique," she said.

Reek read with the actors, part of his job. He hated it, too, you could tell. Now he glared at Em. While everyone else laughed.

She said, "I'm serious. You were better than any of them, Reek."

The Scarf started to say something but Mike stopped him. He said, "You know, that's not a bad idea." He flung himself back in his chair to take a look at Reek.

Someone said, "He *is* ethnic."

"He's about the right age."

"He even looks a little like Monty."

"Now wait a minute..." Reek tried, but no one even heard him.

Mike looked at me. "What kind of shape is the script in?"

I shrugged. We'd been doing tables all week. "Okay." Mike nodded. He was seriously considering this.

Maybe Em *can* lie.

CHAPTER 45 ◆ I GOT ALONG WITHOUT YOU BEFORE I MET YOU, DOO-DAH DOO-DAH DAY ◆

Reek dropped in around noon. Normally, I hate people dropping in. It's like having your mother phone just when you get out the vibrator; it's all in the timing. When Reek walked up the stairs to my apartment and whistled, I was nursing my third cup of coffee and watching Saturday morning TV, bitter over the pathetic state of animation these days. Reek provided a welcome distraction and some pot.

An hour later, we were working on our tans. He did it all: the guy traveled with folding chaises in his trunk, and since I don't have a backyard per se, he set us up on the roof. There was this fire-escape ladder thing outside my bedroom window—I'd never even thought about going up on the roof. He also brought out the tape player and fixed us cold drinks. I rolled joints. "Very New York," I said as we settled in.

"It's the blacktop," he said, rearranging the towel on his chaise lounge. "We'll get twice as much sun."

I was amazed at his energy. "You're a can-do guy, Reek."

"I clear a path for your creativity."

"Makes you sound like a fucking snowplow." Maybe that's what he does for Mike, I thought. He always seemed to be hovering around. "Is that what you do for Mike?" I asked. "Clear a path for his creativity?"

"More or less. Or is it more *and* less? You white people have such strange expressions."

"I love the way you're selectively ethnic, Reek. It's one of my favorite things about you."

He ignored me. "People like you need people like me."

"Didn't Barbra Streisand say that?"

He didn't miss a beat. "*I* said that. Look, let me put it this way. People like you *think* they need people like me."

"And people like *you* like to think there *are* people like me."

"I know there's no one like me."

"Thank God." I couldn't resist.

"That's it, take my drugs, treat me shitty."

I murmured something; I'd forgotten what it felt like to relax. It was an absolute luxury to lie there and do nothing but sweat.

"By the way," he said, "I should be mad at you. This acting thing is all your fault."

"Not *all*." It was Mike's decision to cast Reek as Morty. I just wanted to show Bud I could play with the big boys. So when we were in the commissary—Mike, the Scarf, the whole bunch—I said I thought of all the actors, Reek was the one who read best. And Mike jumped on it. It was supposed to be a joke, the Casting Director being better than the so-called talent. But now Reek was taking it seriously and Bud was pissed.

I said, "So you're really doing it? Changing careers? Becoming a star."

He missed the sarcasm. "Are you kidding? After the deal I cut? Which, by the way, is the only reason I'm still talking to you. God knows, the work is going to be hell."

"Why?"

"Because the cast all hates me. They consider me a spy for Michael."

"Are you?"

"Of course. But I'm not happy about it."

I shook my head; he was such a mass of unconscious contradictions. In fact, as I watched him slosh on more Hawaiian Tropic, I couldn't help thinking how most people would kill to have his skin, deeply bronzed and without a line. The truth was though, in Hollywood a tan like that was only good if the skin underneath it was white.

"You want to know a secret, Emmaline?" He didn't slow down enough for me to say no. "I've always wanted to be a star . . . Let this be a lesson. Watch what you wish for; you may get it." He began telling me about his deal with Mike. I half-listened, concentrating on the red spot the sun made behind my eyelids.

Around four o'clock, we came inside. Reek immediately opened the fridge. "By the way," he asked, "where's Bud? I thought I was gonna catch you two at it this morning."

I snapped. "Reek, are you still spreading rumors about Bud and me? Because if you are, you're in serious fucking trouble. I have a friend who's large and mean, and he would gladly break both your knees with a baseball bat." Bud had left work early yesterday, right after lunch. He'd mumbled something about being busy all weekend.

Reek changed the subject. He was what you'd call *adept* at changing the subject. "So what've you got to eat around here?"

I wanted him to leave. I felt restless and irritable. I said, "Don't you have someplace to go, Reek?"

"Listen," he said, turning from the open refrigerator, "I don't mind if you call me that, but don't do it in front of other people anymore. Murray the Scarf asked me thirty times what it meant. And light that joint. It'll get rid of your headache."

Sunday, I went to Bullocks Wilshire, mostly to get out of the house. I bought Claire another blouse and three pairs of shoes for myself. Then, feeling guilty about giving Reek a hard time, I bought him a silver frame. When I got home I fitted a piece of paper into it that said *Your 8 × 10 Glossy Here.* I even gift-wrapped it.

Monday morning, I was up at 7:00. I read the paper and drank coffee. I finally couldn't stand it any more and left. I got to the lot at a quarter to ten. Reek wasn't even in yet; I left the present on his desk.

I went upstairs. Our office was empty, too. I opened the venetian blinds, and as I turned around, I saw this package on my desk. Of course, we only had one desk now, and whoever had dropped the package off might not know it was mine. I looked closer: it was Bud's sweater, his white cardigan with the cables, wrapped in a plastic bag. There was a red paper band around it that said *Inter-Office Delivery.* There was also a note.

"*Dearest Bud, Thank you for the weekend. It's the best gift you could have given me, and only you had the ...*" I had to move the red paper band to see the rest, which read, "*. . . power to give it to me.*" It was signed "*Love, love, love, Joyce.*"

Who the fuck was Joyce? It was sent inter-office, so she must work on the lot. *Love, love, love?* Obviously not a writer.

"Aren't you going?"

"Huh?" I turned around and there was Peggy, standing in the doorway. "Going where?"

"To the reading." She smiled excitedly.

"What reading?" I casually smoothed Bud's note back into the red paper band.

"With Reek. Your new script. Come on, you don't want to be late to the reading of your own script!"

I went downstairs. I planted a big smile on my face. I couldn't wait to show Bud Goodman how fucking happy I was.

CHAPTER 46 ◆ ANOTHER GODDAM READING ◆

And this was bound to be the worst. This reading was with Reek. Was Mike really serious or what?

He looked serious. Standing there wobbling. Glad-handing the network. Two guys, one girl. Mike had the girl snowed already.

Go eat a doughnut, Goodman. You'll feel better.

I don't think so. My stomach's killing me.

No wonder, all that garbage you ate yesterday. Cotton candy. At your age.

I know. Edna had fun though. She loves that zoo. Which is why I saved it for Sunday. Plus those trains. The model ones. I didn't even tell her about them beforehand, on account of the hobby club that runs them isn't always there. But we got lucky.

It was a great day. Sunshine. Nice breeze. None of that Santa Ana crap either, a real breeze. We rode around on the trains, seemed like hours. They're models but they're big enough to ride around on. If you call a chubby guy hanging over the rails riding. Edna loved it.

Afterwards we went over the hill to C. C. Brown's for hot fudge sundaes. I guess it was a long day, she fell asleep on the drive back out to Malibu.

When I got to Gordon's, he and Joyce weren't back yet. It was their honeymoon. That's why I was taking care of Edna, so they could get away. Big Spender Gordon took her to La Jolla for the weekend. Hell, even I took her to Tijuana.

I wasn't crazy about leaving Edna there. I mean, Joyce said they'd be back by seven and it was nine already. I almost took her back home with me. But then she woke up. And she said she'd be fine with the housekeeper and Joyce and Gordon probably just lost track of the time. That killed me. What does it say when the kid is more grown-up than the grown-ups?

"Must've been a helluva weekend."

It was Tony Wayne. He was standing there with that other guy, the junior genius film editor.

I said, "Tony Wayne, the man with two first names."

He said, "Look at that smile, Rob. That is the smile of a man who got laid."

These guys, all they ever think about is sex. I said, "I'm thinking of becoming a priest. That means no sex unless they assign me to a parochial school."

"Are we actually going through with this farce?" That was Arnie Dish. I turned to look at him just as Emmaline came in. I waved at her.

"What makes it a farce?" That was the editor talking.

"Enrique Carlos?" Arnie said. Really laying it on. "In the lead?"

I looked around for Reek. He didn't seem to be here yet.

Then Tony said, "I heard Monty wants more money and the network expects Mike to pay it."

"Is that true?" Arnie Dish asked me.

I said, "Hey, I'm a writer. I don't know anything."

Then Reek came in. And Arnie Dish says, "Look, the star's here."

Reek was wearing a blazer, for pete's sake. I figured I better say something. Insult him in a joking way. Before these guys did it in a serious way.

So I said, "Reek! We all want to know. Are you the permanent spic or the substitute spic?"

"He's the spec spic." That was Em. She had her hand on his arm.

And Reek said, in his fake accent, "Wha's that? He wants to spic to my pipple?" Which was good. To make a joke out of it, I mean.

Then Ronnie came over. She kissed Reek on the cheek and said, "It's nice to have you with us, dear." She was very classy, Ronnie. And none of the guys messed with her either. Even Arnie Dish.

Mike came in about ten-fifteen with Murray the Scarf. They finally got everyone settled down and we started the reading.

It was okay. Reek was nervous but he did all right. He even got a couple of laughs. Plus which, the scene we added with Adalbert in the candy store worked. He's been around forever and he knows what to do with his lines.

The rest of the cast started in as soon as we finished the reading. Arnie Dish claimed the new character was extraneous. Tony Wayne said he had nothing to do. Even Chip wanted to know where all the jokes were and he's just a kid. Mike kept nodding and listening and looking like he was taking it all seriously. The reading didn't really end, it just kind of fizzled out. The network left and Mike said there'd be a writers' meeting at 2:00.

I went upstairs. I figured I'd call Joyce and make sure she got back and Edna was okay.

Emmaline was sitting on the couch. "Hi," I said. I picked up the phone.

"Aren't you going to check on your package?" she said, pointing at her desk. I hung up the phone without dialing.

It was my sweater. I forgot, Edna wore it home last night. Gordon must be working on the lot; he sent it over inter-office. I ripped open the plastic bag and a piece of paper fell out.

"Dear Bud, Thank you for the wonderful . . ." I kind of skimmed over it. Emmaline was watching me and I felt kind of funny. For some reason, I don't know, I said, "Returning my sweater. She wore it home."

"She must have looked adorable."

I thought I was used to Em being sarcastic. I mean, most of her jokes are in the sarcastic vein. But I don't know, there was something different about this. I said, "What are you talking about?"

She said, "Your date. She must have looked adorable in your sweater."

My date? "Em, this is about Edna. Joyce's kid."

It finally sunk in. Took a while. "Edna?"

I said, "Joyce's kid. My third wife."

"Ex-wife."

"Yeah. I was baby-sitting. Joyce and Gordon got married. They went on a honeymoon to La Jolla, and Edna and I . . ."

She said, "Why didn't you tell me?"

I said, "I don't know." The fact of the matter is, I didn't like any of the crap she pulled on Friday. Trying to out-do the Mogul, pushing Reek like that. I didn't want to talk to her. I didn't want to be around her, and I didn't want to see her. I didn't say any of that, of course.

She said, "I didn't even know you like kids."

Women never think guys like kids. I said, "I love kids. Some kids. Edna."

She put both her hands on my face. She said, "You're so corny. That's why I love you."

Before I got anything out, she said, "And because you're a great fuck." Then she kissed me fast, on the lips.

I . . . I've . . . got to think. Did she say what I think she said?

Think later, Goodman. Kiss now.

That was the trouble with Em, I was always going to think later. Who was I kidding? It was already later.

CHAPTER 47 ◆ WHAT DO I DO NOW? ◆

I love you. I love you. Why did I say it?

Maybe he didn't hear me. Maybe he didn't notice. I tried to cover up by saying *And because you're a great fuck.* Maybe that distracted him. Men are fixated on sex.

I went to the two o'clock meeting. I purposely took a seat where I couldn't even *see* Bud without turning around in my chair. Not that it mattered. I couldn't think about anything else anyway. Mike mumbled on and on about how unhappy the actors were and how fundamentally flawed the second act was, and I barely bothered to take notes. After a while, Mike and Bud went into some special closed-door session in Mike's office.

At the end of the day, I wandered back to our office. Bud still hadn't surfaced. I *had* to say something. What? *I know I said I love you, but I didn't mean it? Or, I meant it, but you don't have to say anything back.* Shit. I went home.

Tuesday morning the writers were already in the conference room when I came in. Bud was at the head of the table; he looked at me and for a minute, I thought everything was going to be okay. Then he looked down and shuffled some papers in front of him. The seat at the foot of the table was vacant, but I took a side seat instead. I didn't want to be constantly looking at Bud *not* looking back at me.

"I don't see why they hate him so much," Nyles was saying. He was talking about Reek, of course.

Rudankowitz said, "I think it's funny."

"He's not that bad," Nyles went on. "Besides, if we eliminated *all* the assholes in town, who'd do the acting and directing?"

"Or the writing?" I said. Bud glanced up, his eyes pained.

"They sure do hate him," Neiderhoff said happily.

"I wonder why," said Rudankowitz, sharing his glee.

"Maybe he tried to poison their doughnuts," I said.

Rudankowitz rubbed his fat hands together. "Speaking of which, why don't we send a gofer over to the commissary for some Danish?"

"What'd you say?" Bud asked.

"I said, let's send a gofer over to the commissary . . ."

"Not you. Emmaline. You said he tried to poison their doughnuts."

"I said *maybe* he tried to poison their doughnuts. I was attempting to be humorous. Obviously, failing."

"What if he did? Morty. Poison them." Bud waved his hand impatiently. "The tuna fish story."

It was an idea I'd pitched for Pops; he gets two cans confused and makes a tuna casserole out of cat food. It was variation on a plot that's been done a million times, although I don't think that's why Mel shot it down. "It might work," I said.

"Scene one," he started, "they all reject him . . ."

I couldn't help myself; I started pitching back. "But Morty wants them to like him. So he invites them over for dinner . . ."

"A home-cooked dinner," Bud interrupted, smiling. "Because he's a cook."

I nodded. "Scene two, he cooks the casserole. Which he calls Tuna Surprise."

"As in, Surprise if there's any tuna in it."

"Perfect. Good Arnie line."

"Right." He scribbled a note. "Scene three, they eat it, love it. They ask for seconds. "

"Thirds. Pete licks his plate."

"It has a unique, delicious taste."

"They can't stop raving."

"Then the discovery . . ."

"That it's cat food . . ."

He nodded. "Act two block comedy scene. They all get their stomachs pumped."

"That's funny. And Pops can be the one who realizes it's cat food. Because he sometimes eats it himself.

Although if that's too harsh, he can have a friend who eats it. To make ends meet."

Bud was nodding again. "Plus which, he can't see what they're all upset about because this is obviously the expensive brand."

"In the end, they wind up...what? Accepting him?"

"But threatening to kill him."

"In a future episode," I said, smiling. Then we stopped, and I realized no one else had spoken during the whole run. We didn't need anyone else. Even if we can't be lovers, I thought, we can still write together.

We ran it down again and Bud assigned the scenes. Everyone had left to write when I realized we'd lost the phone booth scene. I loved that scene. I mentioned it to Bud, who reshuffled papers and said, "We could stick it in Act One."

"Lucky gives Morty the idea for the dinner?"

"Yeah. You want it?" he asked.

"Sure. Thanks, Bud."

He nodded, and as I stood up, he said, "I still have to put it all back together. Would you help me?"

"Sure. Just because we're not sleeping together doesn't mean we can't write together."

"I'll work in here," he managed.

I was coming out from the bathroom when Reek stuck his head out of his office door. "Pssst," he said. The lobby was empty. Even Sahndra was away from her desk. "Get in here!"

"What's the matter?"

He pulled me into his tiny room and shut the door. "I heard you guys are doing a whole new script!" His voice was low and urgent, his eyes wild. "You have no idea what it's like working with these people. They hate me. They drop their cues, leave me hanging, anything to make me look stupid! And now you want me to memorize a whole new script!"

"Actually, Reek, it's a much better story."

"Did you hear that?" he interrupted frantically. He stood frozen, straining. After a moment, a toilet flushed. His office was strategically located between the two bathrooms.

"I think it's just someone peeing."

"Shhh! There!" His finger jabbed the air. I did hear faint voices.

"Who is it?" I whispered.

"Probably that little shit, Arnie Dish. You should hear the things he says about me!" His indignation was practically tangible. "He claims I'm running to Michael!"

"Are you?"

"No! Michael won't see me anyway." He suddenly crumpled. "He's gonna hang me out to dry, I know it."

"Come on, Reek. You can't let those old Jews get you down." It was a desperate move on my part, but he took the bait.

"What old Jews?" he asked.

"The ones who run show business." He almost smiled. "And you certainly can't let a schmuck like Arnie-fucking-Dish get the better of you."

"You're right!" He suddenly un-crumpled. "You're fucking right! Why should some lame bunch of actors get over on me? Damn straight!"

I was amazed by the power of my argument.

"When's this dazzling new script going to make its appearance?"

"I don't really know. Bud and I are putting it together later. I assume you guys'll get it tomorrow."

"But I'll know all about it!" His eyes were focused and confident. "Plot?" he demanded. I filled him in; it didn't take long. "Perfect! Now we'll see who has the upper hand!" He adjusted the collar on his sparkling white shirt, then smoothed down his shiny black hair. He opened the door with a flourish. "Information," he said, "is power!"

"Well, and sometimes it's just information." He didn't hear me though; he was already gone.

Bud and I worked on the script; it went well. We worked smoothly together, and I don't think either one of us noticed how quickly the time passed. Peggy came in at some point with pizza, and a little bit later to say she'd made fresh coffee. We finished just before midnight. "I think it's funny," I said. We could hear Peggy laughing while she typed.

"Yeah." Bud stuck his finger into his empty pack of Kools.

"Here," I said, handing him my box of Marlboros. "It feels good to move." I stretched, then felt suddenly self-conscious, as if I were flirting with him. I *was* flirting with him. I wanted him to come home with me.

"Well," I said.

"Yeah. Time to get going."

In bed alone, it took me a long time to fall asleep. I kept thinking about something Bud said to me, Jesus, it seemed like a million years ago. "Don't mess up what we have," he'd warned me. It looked like that's exactly what I'd done.

CHAPTER 48 ◆ DID SOMEONE HERE
ORDER A CHICKEN? ◆

Everyone liked the script. We got a note from Murray, a scarf note, but nice, how the cast especially liked all the mean things they got to say to Reek.

No reason why they shouldn't like it. We did a good job. Too bad I didn't care.

We were following Mike's directions, a table every afternoon. There wasn't much writing to do. A couple of jokes to fix, a few lines to switch. That left the mornings to kill. I guess some of the other writers were working on new stories. Me, I just sat around on the couch.

> In *MindReaders*, his latest novel, Bud Goodman takes an improbable story and turns it into an unfathomable one. People can't read minds; discerning readers won't even make it through this book. If ever a more boring hero lurked in the annals of literature, I don't know my Oliver Twists. Hopefully, Mr. Goodman will indulge in a creative writing class soon. Or perhaps a nap . . .

Goodman, you're spineless.
Yeah. It's one of my best features.
How hard can it be to say? I love you.
Not hard. Impossible. Linda—my first wife—and I, we used to say *I love you* twice a day. Every morning and every night. Seems like she always had toothpaste in her mouth when she said it. *I love you, too*, I'd say

back. We wouldn't kiss, of course. On account of the toothpaste.

Isabelle and I—well, it's not worth thinking about Isabelle. But we sure never said *I love you.* I could never even ask her if she loved Harry.

Joyce and I, we made a deal not to say it. We'd both been around. We figured that a good friendship, not great but good, and good sex, not great either, forget all those belly-dancing stories, we figured that was enough for a marriage. Sometimes I call Joyce the eight-week-wonder. That's how long it lasted. We never said *I love you,* but we sure said *I hate you.* Week number seven.

Now Em was going to hate me because I couldn't, didn't, say it. I wonder if we've known each other seven weeks already.

"Jesus, this place sucks." It was Emmaline, standing in the doorway, a cigarette dangling out of her mouth.

"Like a hotel maid," I said before I thought. Em's eyebrow went up. "Like a hotel maid vacuuming, I mean."

She flopped down on this purple hassock we'd brought up from the warehouse. It had wheels, and when she first got it, she used to push herself all around the room on it. Now she just sat there.

She wore a long ruffly skirt and her toenails were painted lime green. When she sat down, she pulled up her skirt. You couldn't see her underwear or anything but you could see her knees. Sometimes knees are pretty sexy. I don't mind saying I missed, you know, messing around with her.

I'd picked up this brochure. At a travel agent near my house. I walk by it on my way to Tiny Naylor's, where I've been eating a lot lately. The brochure's for Portugal. Six pages of color photos, map included. The captions say things like *Breathtaking views! Fresh fruit all-year round! Quaint bazaars!* I had this crazy idea about Em and me going off together.

"You got a match?"

"Yeah." I took a pack of matches out of my pocket. Tiny Naylor's. "Em," I said before I could stop myself, "there's something I've been meaning to show you . . ."

The door swung open and Reek walked in. "What are you two doing?" he said.

Em glanced at me. "You know, we've got to get an alarm for that door."

I nodded. "Maybe something with an electric shock hookup."

"I'm very amused," Reek said. "Why aren't you ready for the meeting?"

"What meeting?" we said at the same time.

Reek said, "You two are getting weirder and weirder. The meeting Mike called. Come on!" He was already pulling Em up, and he looked at me impatiently. "Let's go!"

"How do you know we're supposed to go?" she said. "No one told us about it."

I said, "That's how you know you're out of the loop. They stop telling you where the meetings are."

I meant it as a joke, but they looked at each other like it was serious. As we walked, Em said to me, "You were going to show me something?"

I felt the edge of the brochure in my pocket. "It can wait."

How long before fresh fruit goes bad?

CHAPTER 49 ◆ YOU ARE WHAT YOU WEAR ◆

Bud and I were the only two writers at the meeting. The cast was there, and Murray the Scarf, and Michael was conferring off to the side with Katrina Rhinestone. His head swiveled around to look at us, and he rocked from side to side. "I'm glad you could join us," he said.

"Thanks for inviting us," I responded sourly. Fucking Mogul.

We sat around the mocked-up set of the candy store. Except for Mike, who lurched around the rehearsal hall in front of us. "I know I haven't been able to give you my full attention," he began. "Unfortunately, I've had to devote time to other projects. And I know this show has, as a result, suffered. But now I think," his head twitched to the side as he added, "we are right on track."

Tony Wayne was sitting on the stool next to me. "He's going right on back?" he asked.

"Right on track," I corrected in a whisper.

"We have a good script," Mike continued. "Once again, our writers have come through." He gave a jerky nod at Bud, who was staring at his feet. "And at last we've solved our casting problem." This time, he nodded at Reek.

"Some people think," Arnie Dish said, not quite under his breath.

The Mogul looked at him sternly. "I know you're going to do our play justice. And now I'm going to tell you your reward." He took one of his patented dramatic pauses, standing as still as he could. "We ... are having ... a *premiere*." He gave the word its full weight, conjuring up movie stars and spotlights sweeping the sky. "A gala. A black-tie bash."

"A back-sty bash?" asked Tony Wayne. I translated again.

"In two weeks," Mike said. "We're going to screen the show at the Preview House. We'll get virtually immediate feedback." He looked very proud of himself, the artist unveiling his latest achievement. "The network is very excited."

"They behind us a hundred percent?" Bud muttered. I think I was the only one who heard him.

"One more thing," Mike said before he let everyone go. "The network doesn't like the name Morty. They say it's not Hispanic enough."

"They're right, it's Jewish," I said.

People laughed and Mike nodded. "Ed Cooper's thoughtfully given us an alternative. Eduardo."

We all hooted; everybody wants to be a star. Only Tony Wayne didn't get it. He said, "El Guard Hole?"

"Eduardo," I said.

Arnie Dish wanted to know if black-tie *really* meant black-tie, and Mike said it did. As they all began buzzing excitedly about what they were going to wear, Mike stood up. "All right, children. Work hard!"

Bud and I fell into place behind him, matching his progress out to the reception area. Katrina Rhinestone was there waiting; when she saw Mike, she ran up the stairs ahead of us. We climbed at a more tortured pace. Mike said, "Let's hope it goes over as well with the writers."

"Why wouldn't it?" I asked.

"They're not as easily distracted by wardrobe," he answered.

The writers bought the premiere without any problem. Nyles talked about the control panels installed in the seats at Preview House. Rudankowitz kept muttering in Pfeiffer's ear, and I noticed when the meeting broke up, they stayed behind to talk to Mike.

I followed Bud into our office automatically; I forgot I'd been avoiding him. I missed hanging out with him. I missed his awful jokes. I didn't want to admit how much I missed sleeping with him.

"Big doings, huh?" I said.

"Yeah." He nodded, peering into a semi-squashed pack of Salems. "I don't have to tell you this is probably just a new mogul move."

That afternoon, I went back to Bullocks Wilshire. I tried on a Valentino and an Ungaro. Normally, I'd never think of spending that much money for a dress, but I wanted something special. I bought the Valentino, which was red, and they promised to have the alterations done in time.

I knew Bud had misgivings about the taping, the Mogul, the whole fucking mess. I'd told him I didn't want to hear it and he didn't really want to tell me. Sometimes, when you know a topic's going to be painful, you avoid it to protect each other. And sometimes that's just an excuse; you're really just protecting yourself.

CHAPTER 50 ◆ PARTY PARTY, WHO'S GOT THE PARTY? ◆

I bought a white dinner jacket. I don't know why. I mean, I had to wear something to this shindig. But Em was surprised when she saw me. She didn't know I bought it. She said, "You look like Humphrey Bogart!"

I said, "More like Sidney Greenstreet." She had this thing about *Casablanca*. The truth of the matter is, I did feel pretty good.

But Em, she looked incredible. Her hair had something called highlights. They put red stuff on it, she said. Whenever she was near a light she looked, what's the word? Fiery. Her dress was red, too, cut low in front and off her shoulders, with a skirt that fanned out when she spun around to show it off. And red high heels. "You look like a movie star," I said.

"As long as I don't look like a writer," she said back.

We took her car. She had the top up. I guess she didn't want her highlights blowing out. Preview House is right on Sunset, and when we pulled up, they had the whole thing going. Searchlights, valet parking, red carpet up the steps. Inside they were serving champagne and hors d'oeuvres. I don't know how normal people make do with popcorn.

"It's about time you two arrived!" It was Reek. He was wearing a gold tuxedo jacket.

I said, "You look like Ricky Ricardo's grandson."

He said, "Don't start with me, Bud." Then he gave me the once-over. "The dinner jacket isn't bad."

"I think he looks dreamy," Emmaline said. A waiter came over to us with a tray of champagne. Em raised her glass and said, "To success!"

"Whatever that is," Reek said in a sour voice.

I knew how he felt. We clinked glasses.

Then Reek leaned over to Em. "I have to talk to you," he said. "Now!" And he dragged her off into a corner.

I stuck my hand in my pocket for a cigarette and ran into the brochure for Portugal. I still hadn't shown it to her. I'd been moving it from pocket to pocket. Waiting for the exact, right moment.

The last couple of weeks had been crazy. We were busy around the clock. Writing, rewriting, even hanging out on the set while they shot. Feeding them lines, new jokes. Em turned out to be pretty good with the actors. Reassuring them, that kind of stuff.

I thought it would be hard being around her. And not sleeping with her, I mean. That part seemed to be over. Not that I was sure. Sometimes I'd catch her looking at me. Or standing real close. And I'd think, she wants me to make a move. Only then Reek'd walk in, or Mike, or Murray the Scarf. But maybe when I showed her the brochure . . .

"Is this your idea of an inside joke?"

"Huh?" I turned to see who was talking. Tony Wayne with his sidekick editor pal. They were both holding programs—Mike had these special programs printed up for tonight—and pointing to the new title of the show. *Eduardo, Go Home.*

"More like an outside joke," I said. "Outside chance anyone'll laugh."

"Ba dump bump," said Tony Wayne. Everyone's a critic.

They wandered away and I looked down at the program. *Eduardo, Go Home.* Formerly known as *Morty Strikes Back.* Known before that as *Happy Go Lucky.*

Never trust a script with three names.

CHAPTER 51 ◆ ALL THAT GLITTERS, PART 1 ◆

Reek held me by the elbow and whispered viciously in my ear. "Monty Newman was on the lot today!" His voice was strangled and he was barely holding himself together.

"Come on." I kept my voice low and tried to sound calm. I dragged him over to an empty corner. I said, "Okay. Tell me the whole thing."

Reek looked at me, obviously exasperated. "That *is* the whole thing!"

"Monty Newman was on the lot," I repeated. Reek nodded. "Did you see him yourself, or is this intelligence gathered from one of your sources?"

"I saw him myself!" he hissed. "You think I'd trust anyone else with this information?"

"The point is," I said, "it might not mean a thing. I saw Adalbert on the lot the other day. He was there doing some voice-over."

"Adalbert is an actor. Monty Newman is . . . This is not good. Michael's up to something, I know it."

"You don't know anything of the sort, Reek. You're letting paranoia take over. You're nervous. It's understandable, but you have to get yourself under control."

"You guys find a place to get high yet?"

It was Tony Wayne, hip cocked and hair greased back, smiling that movie-star smile. I said, "Hi, Tony. You look resplendent tonight."

"Yeah. I do look resplendent, don't I?" He was wearing a red lamé jacket, tight black pants with matching red stripes down the sides, and red snakeskin cowboy boots.

"Resplendent, possibly," Reek said. "Subtle, no."

"*Subtle?*" Tony repeated. "Is that the look you were going for?"

Reek's jacket was gold lamé.

"Boys," I said, "make nice. It's a party."

"More like a wake," Reek said with a pout.

I was about to tell him to cut the doom and gloom when a pair of ushers in maroon blazers opened the double glass doors of the lobby. In swarmed a crowd of polyester-clad tourists, most of them with cameras glued to their faces. They stared at the champagne and hors d'oeuvres, craning their necks to search out celebrities. The maroon blazers herded them efficiently into the theater, although a few managed to notice Tony Wayne and snap pictures of him. He waved merrily. "Join in, Reek," he said. "You're being baptized." Reek drained the last of his champagne. "This is the worst night of my life," he moaned.

Poor Reek, I thought. But Tony was relentless. "And it's just beginning," he said with a malignant grin.

CHAPTER 52 ◆ ALL THAT GLITTERS, PART 2 ◆

Emmaline slid into the seat next to me. "You excited?" she said.

"Thrilled. What's with Reek?"

"Oh, you know Reek," she said. "Mini-mogul paranoia." The lights went down and she reached over to squeeze my hand. "This is so fucking cool!" Then she took her hand back.

A special section of the audience was reserved for voters. Their seats had arms holding panels with buttons. They were supposed to hit the buttons every time they laughed or saw something they liked. When it was over, they had to fill out cards. Questionnaires. Like it wasn't bad enough they had to watch the show, they had to take a test on it, too.

Truth of the matter is, the show wasn't bad. At least it was short. Without commercials, half-hour TV shows are only twenty-two minutes long. Most people can sit through amazing piles of crap for twenty-two minutes.

When it was over, the audience applauded. Mike walked out on the stage, and there was that moment of silence while the people who didn't know him got a look at the way he lurched and twitched when he moved. A technician followed him lugging a microphone. A mike for Mike. He introduced everyone. Including us. We even had to go up on the stage.

Em loved it. When Mike invited the whole audience to the party at the Beverly Hills Hilton, she turned to me and said, "God, this is just like going to Sardi's to wait for the reviews."

I was feeling more like Abe Lincoln after John Wilkes Booth. What about *his* reviews?

The thing of it was, I had this idea I'd show her the brochure on the way to the party. And I figured she'd, I don't know, get so excited and be so happy that she'd say, Who cares about going to the party? Then we'd go off and be by ourselves and well, the rest of what I was thinking was pretty much what you'd expect.

Of course, that's not what happened. For starters, she dragged Reek along with us. She put the top down on her car. There's this little area in the back, not exactly a seat, but it was big enough for her to squeeze into. I drove and Reek sat in the passenger seat and she perched in the way-back. "I feel like a homecoming queen!" she said. She stuck her legs out in front of her. Practically in my lap. Every time I shifted gears I almost grabbed a foot. In a red high heel.

"I think it went well!" She had to yell, on account of the noise of the car and the wind.

"How can you tell?" Reek.

"They laughed." Emmaline.

"They were protecting their jobs." Reek.

"Not all of them." Em.

Neither one asked what I thought.

It didn't take long to get to the hotel. Just a fast zip up Sunset. More valet parking, more lights, more show-biz hoopla. Em grabbed hold of Reek on one side and me on the other and led us down the fake red carpet like a movie queen.

I don't know how everybody managed to beat us there, but the room was packed. A bunch of guys with marimbas and ruffled shirts reminded me that the lousier the music, the louder it is.

Right away Em tried to drag us out on the dance floor. "Uh uh!" I said. "No way."

"Thank you, I'll pass." That was Reek trying hard to be dignified. Which isn't easy when you're wearing gold lamé.

"What a pair of wimps." Off she twirled with Tony Wayne.

Reek and I headed for the bar. I don't know, maybe it was wearing that white dinner jacket out of *Casablanca*. Suddenly I had this flash that Reek was Peter Lorre about to get nailed by the Nazis.

Em was having a great time on the dance floor. She and Tony were going at it, and I have to admit, they looked all right.

"What are you grinning about?" It was Reek.

I shrugged. I didn't even know I was grinning. Then, I don't why, I pulled out the brochure. "This," I said.

He took it. "Portugal?"

"I'm thinking of taking a break," I said. "Maybe during hiatus."

He grunted. "If we don't watch out, we may get a permanent hiatus."

"What do you mean?" I took back the brochure.

"I haven't seen Mike in a while," he said nervously. "Have you?"

I shook my head, but then I did. Actually, what I saw was a ripple going through the crowd. I pointed with my glass. "Coming this way," Reek said. "God help us."

It took Mike a while to reach us. You'd see a leg wrench and then he'd stop, talk to someone, nod, laugh. Katrina stuck close by, her hand reaching out automatically to steady him when he needed it. When they finally made it close enough, I yelled, "Hey, Mike, helluva party!"

"Thanks," he shouted back. "Listen, next week I want you over at *Bigelow's Boys*." There was something after that, but I didn't catch it.

"What about *Lucky* . . . won't we be working?" We all still called the show *Lucky*.

Reek leaned in. He's paid to notice things so he said to Mike, "Have you heard something already?"

The Mogul surveyed the room. "I'll make an announcement later. How the screening didn't meet our expectations. You know."

I looked at Reek. His built-in tan disappeared and he took a large gulp of his drink. Just then the song ended and Em came over. She was fanning herself with both hands. "Can I have a margarita, please?" she shouted to the bartender. "What wonderful music! By the way, Michael, congratufuckinglations!" She grabbed him in a big hug, and they almost toppled to the floor, but she managed to keep him upright. "You must feel so proud!"

He nodded, still looking serious.

"I like your hair!" she said. He had it pulled back into one of those little ponytails. Myself, I thought it looked dumb.

Maybe it was Em standing there so happy and Mike letting her think everything was okay. I don't know. I said, "The preview didn't go well."

207

Em took the margarita the bartender held out to her.

Mike said, "We'll talk later. After the party."

"I thought they liked it," Em said. She looked at Reek, who was sweating. And looking around the room.

Mike sighed. He said, "I think our biggest mistake was moving away from that original script of yours. That first act was one of the funniest, best constructed pieces of writing I've ever seen."

"But the audience laughed a lot," Em said.

Mike said, "This isn't the time for postmortems, Emmaline. I know you're deeply, emotionally involved with this show."

"I don't understand." Em. "Is it the network?"

Mike grabbed hold of the bar, his big hand clenched.

"Emmaline, we're all hurt by this. But you have to realize you're not involved in this decision." It was a very, I don't know, businesslike thing to say. But cruel. Then he turned to me. "So, Monday. *Bigelow's Boys*. We'll have a table. I'm thinking the script is basically sound."

"Bullshit."

It was Em. And whether it was because of no music or a lull in the conversation or her voice being extra loud, people turned to look.

I said, "Em, let it go."

She said, "You had it pegged, Bud. Fucking mogul moves. Isn't it?"

Mike said, "Emmaline, maybe you want to save this discussion for . . ."

"Don't give me that fucking mogul-handling-me-bullshit," she cut in. "This is you. Playing with people's lives."

A circle opened up around us, people backing away like you would from any disaster.

Mike's face twitched. Hard to tell if it was just a regular twitch or the beginning of something bigger. His shoulder jerked and he twisted around. Started walking away.

Em said, "Mike. Michael." He just kept walking and she, I couldn't believe it, she took off one of her red high heels and threw it at him.

She hit him, too. Right in the back of his head. Mike staggered and there were a couple of giggles. Smothered immediately. Mike grabbed someone. Steadied himself. Turned around.

She said, "You evil fucking prick."

He smiled, a cool mogul. He said, "Emmaline, if you have a problem with the way I run my show, you know what you can do."

I knew it. He was trying to get her to quit.

She said, "You don't produce television, Mike. You produce paranoia. That's what you should call your company: Paranoid Bullshit Productions."

He put his hands out wide, palms up. Inviting her to insult him more. I tried to keep my voice low. "Em, he wants you to quit. Your contract is solid. He doesn't want to have to pay you off."

She laughed. One of those unfunny, snorting laughs. She and Mike never took their eyes off each other. She said, "That's perfect, isn't it? You know, Mike, you don't have the balls to fire me."

It wasn't a bad line, but his was better.

"You aren't worth firing," he said. He was the mogul, he had the exit line.

What does she expect, Goodman? Looking at you like that?

"What about me, Mike? Am I worth firing?" It couldn't be. But it was. Me. Talking.

209

"Bud." Mike shifted too fast and lost his balance. Clutching at the air like a tightrope walker in a bad circus movie, he went down. The crowd closed in around him, yelling his name, pushing to be the one to help him up.

I guess Mike didn't think I had it in me. Bud Goodman, Hopeless Hack, Talks Back.

I took Em's hand. And we sailed out of there. Sonuvagun.

CHAPTER 53 ◆ I'D SAY I FELT LIKE A KID AGAIN, BUT KIDS NEVER FELT THIS GOOD ◆

I woke up feeling like the luckiest woman in the world. "I feel great," I said.

Bud nuzzled closer, running his hand over my hip. "Mmmmm. You do feel great. "

I turned to look at him, to take his face in my hands and hold it. "You were so fucking cool last night."

He blushed. "It takes two to tango."

I had to laugh. "I mean with Michael. You were my hero, my shining white knight." I was so proud of him, so surprised and proud. "You saved me from the evil prince."

"That's evil *prick* to you."

"God, I did call him an evil prick, didn't I?"

"Actually, I think it was evil *fucking* prick."

Suddenly I had this vision of Sahndra in her hot-pink, jagged-hemmed gown, watching me in horror. "Did he deserve it?" I was beginning to waver.

"Absolutely."

I felt better. "Good." Bud rolled over onto his back, reaching for his cigarettes on the night table. I said, "Hey, I've got an idea."

"What?"

"Let's quit smoking."

He paused, the Kool halfway to his lips. "Why?"

"Well, we've taken this big step. This *huge* step. This could be part of it. A new beginning."

"I guess." He looked longingly at his cigarette.

"Come here," I said. I pulled him over onto me and kissed him. I loved the feel of him, the solidness of him on top of me. He tossed the cigarette over his shoulder.

I love making love in the daytime. I love being able to *see*. I love that feeling of time stopping and waiting for you. It was quiet in Bud's apartment, peaceful, as if nobody lived in any of the apartments surrounding his. Stewardesses, he'd told me once. Gone most of the time.

"I love fucking in the daytime," I said when we were finished, lying there with shiny bellies rubbing together.

"Mmm."

"What're you thinking about?"

"How much I want a cigarette," he said.

"Come on. Let's go take a shower."

I was soaping his back. I asked, "Are you worried about finding a new job?" I knew he was.

He shrugged. "There are always jobs."

"But this was a good one."

"Truth of the matter is, it was a lousy one. Come on, your turn." He took the soap from me, working up handfuls of Ivory-scented lather.

We decided to walk over to Tiny Naylor's for breakfast. I was looking for my mascara when Bud said, "Emmaline, can I show you something?"

"Sure."

He walked toward me, holding a folded piece of paper. When he got closer, it turned out to be a brochure. I opened it up and he came around so he could look at it with me. "It's Portugal," he said. "Here, look at that water. Did you ever see anything so blue? And fresh fruit, all-year round, it says. I know you like fresh fruit. And this castle, see, right there?" He pointed to a rock fortress built on a cliff. "That's a hotel now. It was built in 1246. They didn't even have TV then. What do you think about going? You and me." He looked six years old.

"I think it would totally rock," I said. God, I loved him.

He whooped. He spun around, then he grabbed my hands and laughed out loud. "Hey!" he said suddenly. "We could go now! Nothing to stop us!" he exclaimed. "We deserve a break, need a break, have earned a break." He decided to call the travel agent. He picked up the phone. "It's dead," he said, suddenly quiet.

I saw the cord nearby. "We unplugged it last night, remember?" We hadn't wanted to talk to anybody.

He plugged the cord into the phone, and at that instant it rang. We looked at each other; Bud picked the receiver up gingerly. "Hello?" There was a pause, then he handed me the phone. "It's for you."

It was Reek, his voice frantic. "Emmaline!! What are you doing?!"

"Good morning, Reek. We're about to go have breakfast."

"Emmaline!" he yelled in my ear. "What about the show?!"

"There is no show. We quit."

"You didn't actually *say* you quit."

212

"Jesus, Reek . . ."

"No one heard you say those words, Emmaline."

"Bud, did we quit?" I didn't bother to cover the mouthpiece.

"We have vanquished the dragon," Bud said. I repeated the line for Reek and hung up the phone. It rang again immediately.

"Should I unplug it?"

"Why bother?" Bud said. "We won't hear it."

"It sounds just like him though, doesn't it?" We left, Reek jangling in our ears.

CHAPTER 54 ◆ FLY ME TO THE MOON ◆

We came out of Tiny Naylor's after breakfast and there we were, right in front of the travel agency. The one where I got the brochure. "Let's go in," I said.

We were holding hands, and so Em stopped when I did. "We don't have to do this now," she said.

I knew what she meant. She was giving me a chance to back out was what she was doing. "We'll never be any closer," I said. We both sort of turned and looked in the window. There was a model of the Concorde hanging down in the middle of some fluffy pink stuff. I think it was supposed to be clouds, but it looked more like someone's couch had exploded. The place was called DreamTravel, one word, but with a capital T. "Come on," I said, giving her hand a little tug. She said, "I'm game if you are." Like a dare.

It was a small office, three desks, but there was only one person working. An older woman, older even than me. Her face had that powdery look, and pointy green glasses sat on the end of her nose. The weirdest part was her hair. It had these stiff brown curls and was kind of perched on her head like it was going to fly away across the room any minute. I hoped to God it was a wig.

"Hello," she said in a warbly voice. "My name is Margaret. Please come in and sit down." She pointed to the seats in front of her desk, like we might sit someplace else if she didn't.

"I'm Bud," I said. "And this is Emmaline. Long *I*."

Em gave me a look, but she didn't say anything. Margaret nodded. "What can I do for you?" she said.

"We want to go to Portugal," I said. "Here." I took the brochure out of my back pants pocket and handed it to her.

She opened it up. Smoothed it out on her desk. She seemed to recognize the place because she nodded and smiled. "Ah," she said." This is a lovely hotel. It sits right above this village. Very quaint."

"*Very* quaint?" Em repeated.

For a second, I could almost hear Em explaining to this old bat how something can't be *very* quaint any more than it can be *very* unique. She was going to start giving her notes, for crying out loud. But then Margaret said, "Unspoiled."

And Em said, "Have you been there?"

"A long time ago," Margaret said back. She stared at the brochure, touching it with her fingertips. Her hands shook. Just a little.

I could feel Em about to ask another question, and who knows, maybe Margaret could feel it, too, because all of sudden, she looked up at us, eyes bright and her head tilted so her wig looked even more like it was going to tumble off and she said, "When would you like to go?"

"As soon as possible," I said. Then I looked at Em. "Right?"

"Sure," she nodded. "Yeah."

"It's a little hard to get to," Margaret told us.

"You don't know the half of it," I said.

Margaret looked confused. "It's very remote."

"That's probably why it's so unspoiled," said Em.

"Exactly," said Margaret. That seemed to take care of it, and she swiveled in her chair to face her computer. She typed in something.

I reached for my cigarettes. Naturally, as soon as I did it, I could feel Em looking at me. On account of how we agreed this morning to quit. And at the same time, Margaret looked at me. She pulled open a drawer and took out a big glass ashtray with one of those leather cigarette cases. Hers was light green with gold clasps.

Em put her hand out like a stop sign. "We just quit," she said.

"Right," I said.

"Oh." Margaret froze.

"But you can go ahead," I said.

"No, I couldn't." Poor Margaret, dying for a smoke.

"It's okay," Em said. "We don't mind."

"It's policy," Margaret said. "So many people have quit."

"So many things," said Em.

"We won't be long," I said to Margaret. "Then you can have one."

Margaret nodded, even though you could tell she didn't agree with me. She put the ashtray away in the drawer and turned back to her computer. I looked at Em. She was smiling at me.

"You nervous?" I asked.

"As a matter of fact, I am." She gave one of those little laughs. Like she was making fun of herself.

"It'll be okay," I said. "I love you."

There was this big, hollow bubble of silence as soon as the words came out. I hadn't meant to say it. I mean, I didn't know I was going to. Em stared at me. I stared at her. And Margaret stared at both of us.

Then Em's head dipped down a little. Still looking at me, but like she was waiting for something.

And I said, "I do." It came out sounding so surprised, we all laughed. Em's was breathy, the ha-ha-ha's all rolling together. Mine was more from the nose and throat, kind of a hunh, hunh, hunh. And Margaret's was high and above us, like a birdcall. Comedy of three laughs.

"I love you," I said again, and we laughed even harder. "Sonuvagun."

CHAPTER 55 ◆ I'M IN PAIN, THIS MUST BE LOVE ◆

He said he loved me! Bud said he loved me!

It came out of the blue. There we were in the fucking travel agency, sitting in front of this ancient, antique woman, and he just said it. "I love you." It was so perfectly Bud-like.

Later, after we'd given the travel agent all the information and she said she'd get back to us when the tickets were ready, we left and went back to Bud's place, the Nothing Manors. That's what he calls it. And I couldn't help it, I brought it up. I suppose I wanted to see if he'd really meant it.

"You looked so surprised," I said to him. "You looked as if it just popped out."

"It did," he said.

"Actually, you looked more than surprised. You looked flabbergasted."

"Does it matter?" He frowned. "I mean, does that change it, that I was surprised to hear myself say it?"

"No. Not unless you never say it again."

I tried to make it light, but he knew what I was thinking. He looked me in the eye and he said, "Emmaline, I love you."

"Oh, Bud!" I threw my arms around him. "I love you, too." I better be careful, or I'd be saying it every five minutes. "I'm going to remember this forever," I said.

"Will you?" His eyes were blue and wistful.

"The moment you first said it is emblazoned on my heart," I said.

"It sounds painful." He kissed me again, very softly and sweetly. Then he sprinted toward the kitchen.

"Where're you going?" I followed him around the corner. He opened the refrigerator and pulled out a bottle of champagne. "Ta-daaa!"

"Cool!"

He got down glasses and opened the bottle. As he poured, he said, "Drink up. Henri says he'll water his garden with champagne before he lets the Germans drink it."

"Here's to Paris," I said.

"No," he said quickly. "Here's to Portugal."

"Better." We clinked our glasses and drank.

"Do you really like *Casablanca*?" he asked.

"I love it."

"It's playing at the Beverly Cinema."

"No way!"

"Yes way!"

I laughed, "When did you find that out?"

He shrugged, smiling. "It's been there all week."

"It's a miracle!" It was really only a coincidence, but it felt like a miracle. "Can we go?"

"Why not?" he said. "We can do anything we want."

"Oh God, that reminds me, I called Ken Harris." Bud frowned. "My agent," I explained.

"Oh yeah. What'd he say?"

"He's out of town. And guess what—he went to Portugal! How's that for coincidence?"

The telephone rang and we both jumped.

I looked at my watch. "Probably Reek."

"I'll get rid of him." Bud leaned over to pick up the phone and I let him. I even encouraged him. They say it's all in the timing, and our timing had turned. It wasn't Reek after all. It was the evil fucking prince.

CHAPTER 56 ◆ COME ONNA MY HOUSE ◆

"All he wants is for me to come up and talk to him," I said for the millionth time.

"Bullshit," she said back. "Like fuck that's all he wants."

"Emmaline . . ." Geez, I was tired. I sat down.

She said, "If he wants to talk to you, why can't he do it on the fucking telephone?"

"It's hard to understand him on the phone." That was true, but even so, it sounded lame.

She said, "You know he's up to something. Christ, he's probably figuring out a fucking way to rewrite the goddamn show."

I said, "You know what? You sound like a sailor."

She gave me a look. She said, "I don't remember mentioning any knots."

I said, "You know what I mean. Your language. You ever listen to yourself?"

She said, "You never mentioned it before."

I said, "That doesn't mean it doesn't bother me." It was practically a mogul line. It worked, too. She was quiet. Too long. I took out my cigarettes. An old pack of Kools. "Want one?"

She said, "Thank you, I have my own."

I laughed. Nervous, I admit it. "I see you started again, too."

"Yes," she said. "Obviously promises mean nothing to either one of us."

I didn't know what to say. "This doesn't have to change our plans."

"What plans?"

"*Casablanca*, we can still go." I dug up the paper and found the listing. "There's a second show starts at 9:15."

She said, "It's only a movie, Bud. It's not important."

I said, "It is important. I want to see it, you want to see it."

She said, "I have it on tape. I can watch it any time I want."

"It's not the same." Even without commercials, it's still watching it on a TV. "It's not the same," I said again.

"I'll take what I can get," she said.

Goddam it. "Emmaline, I'm just going to talk to him."

"He's counting on you to cave."

"Thanks a lot. That's great." As if Mike could make me do anything he wanted. "Don't you have any faith in me?"

"Oh, Bud." She put her head down. At first I thought she was crying, but she gave one of those big sighs and said, "Fuck."

I looked at my watch. "Maybe a quick one."

She said, "I could change the way I talk."

She caught me off-guard. "Emmaline . . ." Her face looked so young and so, something else. Innocent.

Then she said, "Please, Bud, don't go up there."

This wasn't fair. "Emmaline, I have to go."

She walked out with me. When we got to the Buick, I said, "Em, I do love you."

"It's getting easier to say, isn't it?"

I said, "Yeah." I almost felt relieved for a second.

"It's still hard to mean," she said.

That hurt, that she couldn't resist an exit line.

You'd think a guy like me, married three times, would know something about women. Know what they want. I don't have the faintest idea what they want. The only thing I know about women is they hate our guts.

I'm not just talking about the last few years either. Oprah Winfrey doing shows on men as scumbags. I'm talking about centuries of hate.

They get back at us though. They make us fall in love with them.

I knew I was in love with Emmaline. I ran a red light just thinking about it. But rotten as it is, being *in* love is the easy part. Because you go from being *in* love to *loving*. That's where they really nail you.

If you're *in* love with someone, you have a fight with her, you say, "Good-bye," it's all over, forget it, you're not in love with her anymore. But if you *love* someone and you have a fight, all you can think of is, "I wonder how long we'll be mad at each other." Or if you're really hooked, "I wonder how long *she'll* be mad at *me*."

I was on Sunset. Right before the turn in to Bel Air. There's a big gate there, probably to keep out the Mexicans. I'd be at Mike's in a minute. What was I going to say to him? When we were on the phone and he asked me to come up, I'd said, "What about Em?" He said, "We'll talk about it." That has to be the deal. If I go back to work, Em goes back to work.

Mike answered the door himself. And before I could even say *Mogul*, he yelled, "Reinforcements!" Too loud. Like he was making an announcement. Like he was talking to someone in another room.

He put his arm around my shoulders. Which is hard for him to physically reach. Plus which, when Mike touches you, you notice how it's like there's electricity running through his body. Only it's all screwed up. Erratic. Erratic bursts of electricity. I walked with him into the living room.

There was Monty Newman. Pouring himself a Perrier.

And Nyles Petersen. Studying some notes on a yellow legal pad.

And Katrina Rhinestone. Looking bored at a laptop computer.

And Mel Biederbeck. Monty's hip-pocket head writer. Back for another round.

For crying out loud. It was a rewrite.

CHAPTER 57 ◆ I HEAR FROM MY FRIENDS THAT HE HATES ME ◆

Bud went up to Mike's house. Nothing I said made any difference, he wouldn't change his mind. The fucking Mogul phoned, and Bud had to go. He said he loved me and I said, "It's getting easier to say and harder to mean." Shit.

A long time ago, I'd asked him, "Do you believe in romantic love?"

"I believe in *rheumatic* love," he'd said. "Love is sick." I should've paid attention.

<u>Love is the biggest lie of all.</u> If you believe in love, you go out and buy chocolates, flowers, Valentine's Day cards. You swallow all that happy-ever-after bullshit. You read books like *Wuthering Heights* and you pretend love can last an eternity. Shit, it can't even last a whole TV season. Love was invented by Hallmark and *Wuthering Heights* is just a book. Never trust a writer.

I sat on my sunporch and rolled a joint. I went into the bedroom and got a suitcase out of the closet. I lit up.

Then I heard a car. I ran back to the front door, thinking, It's going to be okay now, Bud's told the asshole good-bye. He's my hero and love *does* exist.

It was Reek. "You look terrible," he said.

I headed for the bedroom, knowing he'd follow me.

"What's all this?" He waved his hand at the suitcase and the clothes on the bed.

"I'm packing. Which one of these blouses do you think I should take?"

"What do you mean *packing*? Where are you going?"

"I thought I told you, Portugal. This one's more practical, but I like this color better."

He said, "I suppose you know Nyles Petersen is up there."

"You're right, I'll take them both."

"Emmaline! *They're* at Mike's writing and *you're* here looking at blouses. They're writing a new show!"

I couldn't breathe. Shit. "You know what's weird? I can only find one of my new red heels."

"You threw the other one at Mike," he said.

I sat down on the bed. God, I thought, I really do *not* want to cry in front of Reek.

"May I?" he asked. He was holding up the joint I'd left in the ashtray. I nodded, trying to avoid eye contact. "Emmaline, are you okay?"

He actually seemed worried.

"I'm fine."

"And Bud?"

"Bud can do what he wants. We're both grown-ups. That's it. Really."

"Of course it is. Here." He held out the joint to me.

"I've had enough. In fact, here, take it all." I picked up the baggie and handed it to him.

I think it was giving him the dope that convinced him I was leaving. "I can't believe you're walking away from the show," he said. "You fought for every word in it. It's made you a very powerful lady."

I looked at him, poor fucking Reek. Poor fucking me. "Enrique, I am *not* powerful. I was *never* powerful. I was just another asshole."

"And how much fun is Portugal going to be all by yourself?"

"It'll be a lot better than this place."

He sighed. "Well, you've got that right." He sat down heavily in the armchair. It would be even harder to get rid of him now.

"What about you?" I asked. "Where are you in all this?"

"I may be out of a job completely. Monty's back in the show, I'm out."

"Monty's back?"

He nodded. "And I hear from my friends that he hates me. "

I could've laughed *or* cried, and the only way to choose would've been to toss a fucking coin. "Well," I said, "I've got a lot of packing to do."

"House don't have to fall on me." He stood up. Then he looked around, stalling. "You want me to come by and water your plants while you're gone?"

"Nah. Let 'em die."

He still hesitated. Finally, he blurted out, "Emmaline, do you want me to quit the show?"

"What for?"

"You know," he said, "loyalty, moral support." He flapped his hands around, obviously confused. A totally different Reek. "I don't know. Aren't friends supposed to make some kind of gesture?"

I felt suddenly tender toward him. His code of ethics was culled from old TV shows. "Enrique," I said, "you'd die if you left show business."

Naturally, he took it the wrong way, bristling. "I could find other work. Michael isn't the only game in town."

"Of course he isn't. But he'd be lost without you. Everyone would be."

He cheered up at that. "You never did fit in over there, Emmaline. You're much too classy."

I smiled. "Bye, Reek."

"Bye, traitor."

We didn't hug; everyone in Hollywood hugs, but we didn't.

It was 9:15; *Casablanca* was starting.

My problem, I told myself, is I'm in love with Rick Blaine. I love the gruffness that hides his tenderness, and I love the anger that hides his pain. I love the way he picks up the glass on the table after Peter Lorre knocks it over trying to escape. I love the way he looks at Ilse and thinks she's the most important thing in his life. Shit. Love is so easy in the movies.

I washed my face with cold water. That's what my father always made me do to stop crying.

I told Bud I would change. I don't even know if I could. The French have a saying: Plus ça change, plus c'est la même chose. The more things change, the more they stay the same. The French understand everything. God, I wish I were French.

Merde.

CHAPTER 58 ◆ WHO KNOWS? ◆

Sometimes I say something over and over in my head before I get around to saying it out loud. Sometimes I never say it out loud.

"Mike, I've got to go." That's all I'd have to say. "Mike I've got to go. I have a previous appointment." Perfect. But it wouldn't come out.

The rewrite was more like a brand new show. The character Em and I came up with—Happy/Morty/Eduardo—he was out, natch. Because Monty Newman was back.

Come on, Goodman, you knew all along your script was a set-up.

Yeah, well . . .

There you go, being eloquent again.

The new script centered on Ronnie, who plays Betty. Turns out she has a niece, Shirley. Shirley wants to get married, only she's got no prospects. So Monty sets up husband auditions. That's the big block comedy scene in Act Two, guys auditioning. Only they don't know what they're auditioning for. Which is supposed to make it funny. We could've stolen something better out of *TV Guide.*

Monty loved it. He said, "The great thing about this story is it's Ronnie's. They all love Ronnie. No one'll give us any noise." The story must've been his idea.

Nyles said, "We forgot about Adalbert. He's got nothing to do here."

Monty shrugged. "Think of something then. Goodman, you're good with Adalbert. What can he do?"

I said, "What if he says, Hey, where's that Mexican guy who was here a minute ago?"

They all stared at me. Then Mike said, "Pops can give advice to the auditioners."

Monty goes, "No, that's shit." He was still glaring at me. Then he said, "I got it, he can do an old vaudeville bit. Bud can write him some old jokes."

Mike said, "That's funny."

Bud can write him some old jokes.

"Mike, I've got to go."

Mike's head jerked up and he fell back against the cushions on the couch.

I said it again. I said, "I've got to go." It was easier the second time.

He said, "Oh. You know where it is, Bud. The end of the hall."

I said, "No, I mean I have to leave. Previous appointment." Close enough. I stood up.

Monty said, "What's going on? I thought we were here to work."

Mike looked worried. He said, "Let's take a short break." He stood up, too.

Monty put down his pencil. Making a big deal of it. He said, "Okay. I've got to take a piss anyway." Classy guy, Monty.

Mike took me into his library. I remember the first time I saw it, he told me, "Every mogul should have a library." It has these floor-to-ceiling bookshelves with elaborate moldings, and the books are all leather with gold titles. Only they're fakes. He bought them off a movie set.

He closed the door behind us and said, "Okay, Bud. What's up?"

Who knows why something pops into your head, right? But all of a sudden, I thought of Benny Funt. I said, "Hey, Mike, you remember Benny Funt?"

He said, "Bud, I haven't got all day. You saw how Monty is."

"You've got to remember Benny. He was a ventriloquist."

"What's he got to do with . . ."

I said, "He had this show. Back in the late seventies." I never realized how easy it is to interrupt Mike. "It was called *I'm No Dummy*. Remember? It wasn't very good. I know, I worked on it." I'd forgotten. I was thinking I'd only ever worked for Gene Muncy and Mike. I forgot all about Benny.

Mike said, "Bud, if you have a . . ."

"Benny was a wildman. Always threatening to walk off the show. One night we're having a table. Benny's screaming and yelling like always. Only this time he's screaming we gave all the funny lines to the dummy. Is that great or what? He was serious, too. He wanted the producer to fire all the writers and hire new ones. Because the dummy had better lines than he did."

Mike was quiet. Resting maybe.

I went on. "So he's raving, Benny is, and he makes this ultimatum. If we don't stop giving the jokes to the dummy, he's going to walk off the show. Then he sits down. It's real quiet. And I say, Let's hear what the dummy thinks."

Mike laughed. A sort of a *Hah!* sound.

"The point is, Mike, I've been fired before."

He said, "You aren't fired. I want you back. Monty wants you back."

Monty. I said, "What's he doing here anyway?"

Mike half-sat, half-fell into a chair. "The network gave him creative control."

"And you let them?"

He looked tired. "Goddamn it, Bud! If *Lucky* folds, I've got nothing. You saw what a piece of shit *Bigelow's Boys* is. Which reminds me, you owe me on that. I need you at the table next week. Help them out."

I said, "What about Emmaline?"

He said, "That's out of my hands, Bud. Monty wants her out. You know how that goes. You know the score. You're a pro."

228

"You mean I'm a hack."

"What's the difference? Monty's not comfortable with Emmaline."

"Which you knew all along he wouldn't be."

He turned his hands palms-up, but they wouldn't stay that way.

"You're putting her on *Bigelow's?*"

"Rudenkowitz doesn't want her."

I said, "What about Reek?"

He said, "He'll be taken care of, don't worry."

One more question. "And Ken Harris? Emmaline's agent? You sent him out of town?"

This time he smirked, definitely on purpose. He said, "He did me a favor. I gave him and the wife a little gift." He laughed, then coughed. "I thought you'd appreciate the irony."

I said, "I do. Irony's one of those things writers love. See you around, Mike."

He struggled to get out of the chair. "Don't go, Bud. I need you."

"See what I mean?" I said. "Irony."

"You're right." He straightened up. At least as much as Mike ever straightens up. "I don't need you. I don't need anyone." It came out *ehnnie-uhhn.*

"Maybe a translator," I said.

"You were right, you are a hack. I'll just run over to a used-car lot and get a new one."

"Better yet, have Reek do it."

Mike started giving me hell, and I don't know, maybe it was because I wasn't concentrating. I couldn't catch a word. It was like he was just standing there, spouting gibberish. And it reminded me how in every movie you ever see, there's always that scene at the end, the yelling scene where everybody says the truth

229

they've been keeping to themselves. The goddamn climactic scene. It's always fake and stupid and I didn't want to be in it.

I don't have to do this anymore. Plus which I actually said it. "Mike," I said. "I don't have to do this anymore."

It took him a minute to get out into the hallway after me. But Mike always could yell. Maybe not clear, but loud. And I heard him before I got out his front door. "Goodman," he yelled, "you're a sap!" Or maybe it wasn't him. Maybe it was just the voice in my head.

I made it to Em's house in record time. Ran up the steps. My chest was killing me. I've got to quit smoking.

The door was unlocked. She was in the living room. Sitting on the floor.

"Do you think I'm a sap?" My voice was too loud. And the silence afterwards was too quiet.

She nodded. Then she said, "Thank God." She reached her arms up.

I thought, it must be okay to be a sap. And I kissed her. She kissed me back. If I wasn't careful I'd make love to her right there on the floor.

I said, "Em, there's no telling what'll happen with us. We could be a disaster, a huge mistake."

"Quit being such an optimist," she said. She smiled. That smile that made her look so young. She slid her hand down my back and pulled the shirttail out of my pants. She said, "I was just thinking that maybe we could, you know . . ."

"Em," I started. Then I decided to just say it.

"Em, you're reading my fucking mind."